‡
P935h

How's
Business

HOW'S
BUSINESS

Alison
Prince

FOUR WINDS PRESS

NEW YORK

First published 1987 by Marilyn Malin Books in association with Andre Deutsch Limited, London. First American Edition 1988. Printed in the United States of America

10 9 8 7 6 5 4 3 2 1

The text of this book is set in 12 point Janson.

Library of Congress Cataloging-in-Publication Data. Prince, Alison. How's business / Alison Prince.—1st American ed.   p.   cm.   Summary: A young boy, sent to the country from London during World War II, comes into conflict with some local boys who find ways to test his courage.

ISBN 0-02-775202-X

[1. England—Fiction. 2. World War, 1939–1945—England—Fiction.] I. Title.

PZ7.P9358Hoc 1988 [Fic]—dc19   87-38142 CIP AC

◆

This book is a very special one to me, because I wrote it in collaboration with twenty-one coauthors aged between seven and eleven, whose names appear below. They are the children of Horbling Brown's Church of England Primary School, Lincolnshire, and they are responsible for most of the plot and the characters in the book, as well as that indefinable thing which may be called its "feel."

The book would not exist without Geoff Swallow, Literature Officer of the Lincolnshire and Humberside Arts Association, who thought of the coauthorship idea and made it a reality by engineering a long-term residency at the school. I owe to him a debt of thanks and admiration, as I do to Christopher Gudgin, the Headmaster of Horbling School, and his wife, Denise. Their marvelously perceptive cooperation has added immeasurably to the book and to the enjoyment which the children and I have shared in the writing of it.

My thanks are also due to Marilyn Malin, who gave us a contract to publish the book as an act of wonderful faith before so much as a word had been written. I am grateful as well to the many people who have helped with their knowledge of the district and their memories of wartime experience, to my brother, Rod, for his transport expertise, and to David Mosley of the National Railway Museum for his cheerful and informative letters.

"The angel" is a Roman bronze statuette, found at Tallington and thought to be a charioteer. It can be seen in Stamford Museum.

Alison Prince

Samantha Barber	Wendy Craigie	Lorraine Holmes
Wayne Bowler	Michael Daubney	Michelle Holmes
Simon Boyfield	Michelle Daubney	Gary Howard
Sarah Brackenbury	Giles Edwards	Lisa Howard
Rachel Bristow	Sarah Edwards	Paula Shelbourne
James Casswell	Mark Flear	Ricky Short
Laura Craigie	Daniel Hill	Lisa Wright

ONE

❖

How Grainger lay on his narrow bunk in the air-raid shelter, wishing the morning would come. His blanket made him feel itchy, and he scratched irritably. From the bunk below him, Mrs. Ogden's snores were louder than the thunder of distant gunfire, and the shelter was hot and stuffy. Even after four years of the war, it still smelled of earth and concrete. It also smelled of the Ogdens' fat wire-haired terrier that slept on Doris Ogden's bunk. He was white, with a pink nose and fawn patches on his ears and, as a kind of wartime joke, his name was Bang.

The shelter was very small. How could touch the wall at the end of his bunk with his feet and put his hands on the other wall behind his head without even stretching. But he had grown a lot since the shelter was built four years ago in 1940, between How's garden and the Ogdens', for the two families to use. The hurricane lamp, turned low, hung on its nail by the doorway, which was curtained by a thick blanket in case any light should be seen by the enemy aircraft above them. The lamp's flame was flickering rhythmically and it made a very faint popping noise. How wondered if it was running out of oil. He wished Mrs. Ogden would stop snoring. He was too hot, and he itched.

He pushed his blanket off and hung one foot over the edge of his bunk, scratching at a particularly itchy patch on his wrist. Sometimes he hated the shelter. In his imagination, he ran up the narrow wooden steps and out of the back gate into the alleyway, down the road to the park—but the park would be bigger than it really was, a great sweep of grass with the sky beyond it. Perhaps, if he ran far enough, he would come to the sea. . . . How turned on his side, and the dream became sleep.

The hurricane lamp was out when How woke again, and the curtain had been looped back to let the daylight in. It was cold now. Mr. and Mrs. Ogden and Doris and Bang had gone, and so had How's mother. He was alone in the shelter. It being a Saturday, there was no need to get up early for school. He scratched idly at his wrist, then inspected it in the gray light, finding two or three lumpy red swellings like mosquito bites. But there weren't any mosquitoes about in early March.

How leaned down to retrieve his woolly siren suit from the spare bunk that his father used on the rare occasions when he was on leave from the Army and came to see them. He pushed his feet through the one-piece suit's elasticized cuffs and pulled it up to thrust his arms into its sleeves. He zipped it up to his neck, put his shoes on, and went, as he had in his dream, up the steps to the garden.

The Graingers' garden, like all the gardens that belonged to the terrace of houses, was a small one, and the earth mound that covered the shelter's concrete roof was the biggest thing in it—a sort of brown igloo whose clods of heavy clay subsoil refused to grow anything. How found a piece of shrapnel half-embedded in the earth beside the path and crouched down to pry out the jagged piece of metal. The house was all right. Although there had been a lot of gunfire last night, no bombs had dropped nearby. The shrapnel was a scrap of exploded shell case from the barrage fired against the raiders. How went on up the path to the kitchen door and opened it.

"Hello, love," said his mother. She was standing at the sink, washing some clothes, with her hair tied up in a scarf.

How put his bit of shrapnel with the rest of his collection in a cardboard box on the shelf under the mantel. Then he said, "Something's bitten me. I was itching all night."

"Oh, no," said Mrs. Grainger. "Me, too." She dried her hands and inspected How's wrist. "Anywhere else?" she asked.

"On my stomach," said How. "And on my legs. Look."

His mother looked. "I think those are flea bites," she said. She sat down at the table and tucked a strand of hair into her scarf absently. Her arms were very thin and her hands were red from the soapsuds. "That's the blooming end, that is," she said suddenly. "Old Jerry

3

and his bombs I can put up with, but *fleas*. It's that blasted dog. They'll have to leave it in the house."

"Doris won't," said How. "She says he's got a right to be safe, same as we have." Doris was about twenty, with pale carroty hair and freckles. She worked in a bank.

How's mother shook her head blindly. Then she buried her face in her hands, and How realized with a shock that she was crying. "Mum," he said awkwardly, "don't." He had never seen a grown-up cry before. After a moment he put his arm around her shoulders. "It's all right," he said. "It doesn't matter." Her damp hands smelled of detergent.

"I know, love," said his mother. "I'm being silly." She groped in her apron pocket for a handkerchief and blew her nose. "What with the rationing," she said, "always trying to find something to make a meal. And working at the factory, and your dad being away—I don't know. But fleas. It makes you feel so dirty." After a few minutes she sat back in her chair and let her hands fall in her lap. "I'm just so tired," she said, and her face crumpled again.

"I'll make a cup of tea," said How practically, and filled the kettle from the tap. His mother blew her nose again and gave a kind of laugh. "You're getting quite grown-up," she said.

How lit the gas under the kettle with a match, then put the spent match in the empty jar with the others. He could see the way Doris felt about her dog, but the idea of fleas really was horrid. "Perhaps we could sleep in the house for a bit," he suggested.

Mrs. Grainger shook her head. "The raids are too bad at the moment," she said. "No, the Ogdens have got to leave that dog indoors."

"Couldn't we spray the shelter with Flit or something?" said How.

"Fleas aren't like flies," said his mother. "Flit's no good. There's Keating's powder, but fancy having to go and ask for that in Woolworth's. Everyone'll know what it's for. And I'll have to wash all those blankets." Tears filled her eyes, and she blinked them away. "Isn't it silly," she said. "A little thing like this. But it's the last straw, somehow."

The kettle was boiling, and she got up and reached for the teapot on the shelf. "You're right," she said. "Nice cup of tea, that's what we want. Cheer us up."

By dinnertime, How's mother seemed more like her normal self, and when they had finished their Spam and potatoes and beets, How went over to see if his friend Clifford Lee was in.

"Ah," said Clifford, opening the door that led to his family's flat above a pharmacy, "I'm glad you've come." As always, his round, bespectacled face was serious. His hair was as fair as How's was dark, and it was cut very short around the sides and back of his head. However, he managed to keep the top of it in a long, floppy cowlick that hung thickly to his eyebrows. "I was just going to the market," he said, "to see if Ernie's got any rolling stock."

"You got some money, then?" asked How. He himself

usually had a shilling or two, but his friend put everything he'd got into his beloved model railway.

"No," said Clifford, "but Uncle Percy gave me a
windup fire engine when he came to stay. Ernie might
swap it."

Clifford's bedroom floor was covered by a compli-
cated Hornby Doublo layout, complete with signal
boxes and footbridges and a turntable, mostly acquired
through a process of exchanging and scrounging. Although How was not particularly interested in railways,
he found Clifford's buying trips intriguing, and he had
come to love the business of buying and selling and
bargaining. "I've got a set of cigarette cards," he said.
"Animals of the World. It's complete."

"Where did you get those?" asked Clifford, pushing
his arms into his raincoat.

"Sally Parsons gave them to me for those bits of fur,"
said How.

"What, those scraps you got last week? Coo, you were
lucky," said Clifford. "The rabbit man gave you them
for nothing, didn't he?"

How nodded. "I'll see if he's there again this week,"
he said. "It might be worth actually buying some. The
girls thought they were really nice—cuddly, they said."

They set off down the street, both of them with their
gas masks slung over their shoulders, past a bomb site
where the tall, mauve pink fireweed had bloomed among
the rubble last summer, and soon came to the line of
market stalls. A lot of the shops behind them were
boarded up, having been damaged or burned out, but

the street was busy with shoppers. A long line stood outside a candy shop, and How hesitated. "Do you think they've got chocolate?" he said. He always carried his sweet coupons with him, just in case.

"Dunno," said Clifford. " 'Scuse me," he asked a woman in the line, "are you waiting for sweets?"

"No, dear, cigarettes," said the woman.

The boys nodded and went on. "Sweets don't usually come in on a Saturday," said Clifford.

"They don't *usually* come in at all," How pointed out. "Only sometimes."

"You know what I meant," said Clifford.

Ernie's toy stall was near the end of the row, past the vegetables and the secondhand clothes and shoes. "Hello," he said when he saw Clifford. "Back again?"

"I wondered if you had some rolling stock," said Clifford. "Freight cars or passenger cars."

"Let's have a look," said Ernie, poking about.

How ran his eye over the assorted secondhand toys, thinking about the things people at school liked. He spotted three tin soldiers, their red tunics a little chipped. John Dwyer collected soldiers, and these would look quite smart if they were touched up with some fresh paint. Clifford was already deep in negotiation over a Fyffes banana wagon and a freight car with Palethorpes Sausages written on it, but Ernie was being awkward about the windup fire engine. "I don't care if it *is* new," he was saying. "Two freight cars are worth more than one fire engine. Ain't you got no actual money?"

"No," said Clifford.

"Too bad, then," said Ernie.

How decided to come to the rescue. Ernie looked doubtfully at the Animals of the World cards, but he brightened up when How offered sixpence as well. "If I can have those soldiers as part of the deal," said How.

"Go on, you'll have me in the poorhouse," said Ernie.

"They're not worth anything," How protested. "They're all chipped."

Ernie sighed. "Proper little skinflints, the pair of you," he said. "All right, then."

Pocketing the soldiers, How went on down the street beside Clifford, who was happily clutching his freight cars. "Thanks ever so much," Clifford said. "I'll pay you back."

"Sometime," How agreed. "No hurry."

The rabbit man, who sold homemade fur gloves, was just packing up to go home. How fished out a halfpenny and tried to look like Oliver Twist asking for more gruel, though he knew his snub-nosed face wasn't a bit pathetic.

"Scraps? I've got a few," said the man. "What d'you want them for?"

"The girls at school like them," said How. "I think they make things for dolls to wear."

The man smiled. "Go on then, son," he said. "Kids don't get much these days. Have 'em." He thrust a newspaper-wrapped bundle of fur pieces into How's arms.

"Thanks!" said How, beaming.

"That's all right," said the man. "I got a boy about your age, only he's down in Devon. 'Vacuated."

"I'd rather be here," said How.

"That's what you think," said the man, folding up the small table he used as a stall. "Wait till there's a bomb with your number on it."

How shrugged. There was nothing you could do about that. Where bombs were concerned, you were either lucky or you weren't. The daylight was beginning to fade and all the stall holders were packing up, to get home before the blackout. It was turning colder.

"Come on," said Clifford. "We'd better be going."

How nodded. "Bye!" he called to the rabbit man over his shoulder, but the man was walking away and did not answer.

"My dad wanted us to be evacuated," Clifford said. "But he couldn't leave London, being an ambulance driver, and Mum said we'd stick together. Jean said she wouldn't go, anyway. They couldn't make her go, she said. She'd walk home."

Clifford's sister was twelve, but even so, How smiled at the thought of her setting out on her own. "It's a long walk from somewhere like Devon," he said.

When How got home, he found his mother cleaning the gas stove. Its various bits were soaking in hot soda in the sink, and she was on her hands and knees scrubbing ferociously at the inside of the oven. She sat back on her heels and looked at him. "We're going away," she said.

9

How was astonished. "Where?" he asked.

"To Auntie Kath's," said his mother, dunking her scrubbing brush in the bucket. "I've had enough. Those Ogdens would try the patience of a saint."

"Did you talk to them about the fleas?" asked How.

"I did," said his mother grimly. "And much good did it do me. Anyone would think I'd accused them of having the plague." She attacked the stove again. "May as well leave the place clean," she said. "I've brought your bed downstairs to the dining room and I'll sleep on the sofa, just for tonight. Keep our fingers crossed."

"We're not going in the shelter?" inquired How.

"We are not," said his mother. "I'm never going in that shelter again, not after what Mrs. Ogden said to me."

"What *did* she say?" asked How, fascinated.

His mother dunked her brush again. "Never you mind," she said darkly. "I've sent a telegram to Auntie Kath to say we're arriving tomorrow. I don't know what they'll do at the factory—we're short-handed as it is. But I can't help it."

How tried to remember which of their relatives was the one called Auntie Kath. "Have I seen her before?" he asked.

"Not since you were small," said his mother. She wiped the inside of the oven, then got up with a little grunt and took the bucket outside to empty it down the drain, the sink still being full of water.

"Mind the blackout," said How, going out beside her and pulling the door shut for fear of any light showing.

Outside, it was dusk, and steam rose in a pale cloud as the hot water from the bucket gurgled away.

"Blasted blackout," said his mother. "I'm sick of this war." But she was more like her usual tough, grumbling self, How was glad to see. He said, "Where does Auntie Kath live?"

"Lincolnshire," said his mother. "Out on the fens. She's married to your dad's brother, Jack. He's a builder, same as your dad, only he's a lot older. There were four sisters in between them." She went back into the kitchen and started on the things in the sink.

How watched her. Except for seaside holidays before the war, he had never been away from home. "How long are we staying?" he asked.

For a moment, his mother did not answer. Then she said, "I'll have to come back the next day. Like I said, we're short-handed at the factory. I mean, it's essential war work, making munitions. They wanted me to come full time, but I couldn't, not with you to look after." She rested her hands on the edge of the sink, looking down at the scummy water. Then she looked at How. "Matter of fact, I had a letter from Auntie Kath last week," she said. "Asking why I didn't send you up there until the war's over. She's suggested it several times. And it really might be an idea, love."

How felt a flush of furious indignation. "You mean I'm going to be an evacuee?" he demanded. "Stuck out in some muddy village?"

His mother wiped the oddly shaped iron bars and started fitting them back into place on the stove. She rinsed the sink when she had finished, wrung out the cloth, and dried her hands. How wished she would say something.

At last she sat down at the table and sighed. "You see, if I was here on my own," she said, "I could work full time. Goodness knows, we could do with the money. And Kitty Armstrong says I can go over to her shelter at night. It's only just across the road, and I think she's a bit lonely now her daughter's joined the Wrens. But I don't know that she'd want the two of us. She's a funny old stick."

How stared at his mother in panic. The thought of being sent away to the unknown countryside was much more frightening than the nightly bombing. He was used to that. Secretly, he almost enjoyed its excitement. He liked the feeling that he was *here*, where everything was happening.

"Kath's ever so kind, love," his mother assured him. "I mean, it's not like the poor little kids who were packed off at the beginning of the war with labels tied on their coats like parcels, not even knowing where they were going. It's your own flesh and blood. It's where your dad's people have always lived."

How dug his nails into his palms. He felt shaky inside. There wasn't going to be time to sell those scraps of rabbit fur—or the tin soldiers. He had a terrible feeling of unfinished business. But this morning his mother had cried, and for a grown-up to cry meant that things must really be bad. She wouldn't send him away unless she absolutely had to. He frowned fiercely. "All right," he said. "Only I want to say good-bye to Clifford first."

"There'll be time tomorrow morning," his mother promised. "Before we catch the train."

How nodded. Then he fled from the kitchen, up to the safety of his bedroom—but the big space where his bed had been taken out was a fresh shock. He had forgotten that his mother had moved it. He trailed down the stairs again and went into the dining room, where his bed was jammed up against the sideboard. Ground-floor rooms were safer than upstairs ones, they said—unless a house got a direct hit. But nothing seemed safe anymore. And where on earth was Lincolnshire?

TWO

◆

So you're Howard," said Auntie Kath cozily. She was very fat. "Well, well, well. There's not much to you, is there?"

Her own son, Stanley, tucked his thumbs into the tight belt between his bulging shirt and his bulging trousers, and looked smug. He was thirteen.

"Never mind," went on Auntie Kath. "You'll sleep easy here—no nasty sirens or bombs. You won't mind going in with Stanley, will you? There's plenty of room for two in that big bed."

How and Stanley eyed each other with hostility. "I don't mind sleeping on the sofa," offered How.

"Oh, no, dear, that's in the living room," said Auntie Kath. "The grown-ups'll want to talk after you lads are in bed. No, Jack's going on the sofa for tonight, and your mum's coming in with me. She'll be off back to London tomorrow."

The house was very small, How thought. It had two poky rooms downstairs, and from one of them a spiral staircase in a cupboard led up to the two equally poky rooms upstairs. There was a narrow kitchen at the back of the house, with a coal-fired stove in it for cooking on, but he had not found a bathroom or a toilet.

As if reading How's thoughts, Stanley said, "The lav's out back."

"It's a proper chemical one," said Auntie Kath quickly. "The sanitation man comes every week to empty it. Not like some of the cottages around here—they've still got outhouses. You brought his ration book, did you, Muriel?"

"Oh, yes," said How's mother. "And he's got his gas mask, of course. And the grocer had peaches in, so I brought you a tin."

"That's nice," said Auntie Kath, rather casually, How thought. Tinned peaches were like gold dust. "Is that right what they say, that you're really short of food in the towns?" she added.

How could see that his mother didn't want to grumble. She lifted her chin slightly and said, "We manage."

Auntie Kath clucked, not taken in. "You poor things," she said. "I can see we'll have to feed Howard up a bit. We don't do too badly here, what with chickens and the odd pig." She chuckled and drew a finger across her throat.

Stanley looked at How and said, "You ever seen a pig killed?"

"No," said How.

"Just you shut up, Stanley," Auntie Kath warned him. Large though her son was, she looked capable of flattening him, and Stanley subsided at once. "All right," he grumbled. "I only asked."

How felt more and more depressed.

Auntie Kath's cottage was one of a pair standing at some distance from the village. Uncle Jack, who turned out to be a small, rather silent man, had a yard behind it with an old barn where he stored building materials and parked his truck. "You're lucky, not being in the Army," How had said to him one evening, and Uncle Jack answered, "Too old." That was the end of the conversation, but How felt a little better. Somehow, he quite liked Uncle Jack.

Auntie Kath had escorted How to school on the first morning. It stood in the middle of the village street, and it seemed very small compared with the one How had gone to in London. He thought everything looked very old-fashioned. The windows were too high up to see out of, and the walls were made of dark wood, thickly varnished. The desks were bolted down in rows, with bench seats behind them. In the playground, the two lavatories smelled indescribably awful. How thought living in the country was disgusting.

"Howard Grainger," Miss Jolly said, entering How's name on the register. Her name did not suit her, How thought. She looked very severe, with gray hair scraped back and pinned into a tight bun. She wore a drooping gray cardigan, and she looked at How over the top of her glasses and said, "We have several other evacuees here, Howard, so you should soon feel quite at home."

"Yes, miss," How said dutifully. But the other evac-uees came from quite a different part of London. They had all come here together, and they knew each other very well. How did not belong with them, because he had come to stay with his aunt. But he did not belong with the village children, either. Even Stanley ignored him, pushing and shouting cheerfully with his friends in the seniors. Stanley had a bike, and a couple of other boys called for him in the mornings after How had set off on foot. How did not mind. He preferred to walk to school on his own. Sharing a bed with Stanley was bad enough, involving playful kicks and pinches and endless ghastly stories of pig killing and of agricultural accidents where people got gored by bulls or run through with pitchforks.

Now, on Friday morning, he was walking across the fen on his own, with his gas mask slung on his shoulder in its cardboard box, on his way to school. He stared around him as he walked. It was horrifyingly open and flat. "Used to be under the sea," Uncle Jack had told him. Maybe fish had swum here, How thought, where the black-earthed fields were now. It seemed quite pos-sible. This morning the mist was so thick that it was almost like walking through water, and the raw cold seemed to penetrate his clothes to touch his skin. His hands and feet were icy, although he wore woolly gloves (lent to him by Auntie Kath) and had thick socks inside his boots. The hedges were black and leafless. Ahead of him, the remains of a lightning-struck tree pointed like a spiky finger into the white sky.

It was awful here, How thought. Bleak and cold and flat. No markets or alleyways, nothing to buy and sell and swap. There was a shop in the village that was the post office as well, and a butcher's where cattle lowed sometimes in the building behind it, and a pub. That was all. And the sky went on and on, a vast emptiness from horizon to horizon. He could see the steeply pitched roof of the school now, a gray triangle among the other roofs of the village, turned into a pale silhouette by the mist. A gap in the hedge revealed a path leading across the field toward it. Auntie Kath had followed the lane all the way to the village street when she had escorted How to school on that first day, and until now he had followed the same route, but this was obviously a shortcut. There were some children halfway across it. How set off along the trodden path behind them, with his hands pushed deep into his raincoat pockets and his chin tucked into his scarf. His gas mask bumped rhythmically against his hip as he walked.

The field had been plowed and left fallow for the winter, and How stared gloomily at the clods of earth. They were so utterly dull, he thought, all exactly the same as each other, give or take the odd stone or tuft of grass. Then he stopped. A piece of stone at the path's edge was different. He picked it up and rubbed the earth off it with his gloved fingers. The stone was just a small slip of a thing, wedge shaped and pointed at one end. Looking at it closely, How saw that it was shaped in a series of planes, as if someone had carved it. The thing was a tool of some sort. How pulled the cuff of his woolly glove away from his wrist and dropped the slip of stone inside, to lie in the palm of his gloved hand. Somehow, the feel of it was a comfort.

As he approached the back gate that led into the schoolyard, How found himself thinking about the unknown person who had shaped the piece of stone. Had he—or she—lived here, in this bleak place, all those countless years ago? There would have been no houses then, no school, no church spire sticking up against the sky. Trying to imagine what it must have looked like, How raised his hand and held it before his face to obliterate the buildings, shutting one eye and squinting at the view with his head on one side.

A group of village boys standing by the gate shouted with laughter at the sight of him. "What's he think he's doing?" said Billy Thrower, a solidly built boy who wore a brown jacket with the sleeves turned back because they were too long for him. "Silly twerp."

"Shading his eyes from the sun," said Roger Bull sarcastically, and everyone laughed again, their breath steaming in the mist.

Billy Thrower's laugh was a kind of raucous hoot that always set everyone else off. "Yes, look, he's going all brown," he said, and hooted again.

How knew it was no use trying to explain. He walked across the playground toward the door.

"You can't go in till the bell rings," one of the girls told him.

"I know," said How a little irritably. "I was just going to stand on the step, that's all. It might be a bit warmer."

They eyed him silently; then a boy called Harry Doggett said, "You staying with Mrs. Grainger?"

"Yes," said How. "She's my aunt."

"Fat old girl, i'n't she," said Harry, and they all went into fits of giggles. How felt very alone. He wished Clifford were here.

Miss Jolly opened the door and said, "Where is Johnny Parfitt?"

"He's got a cold, miss," Billy Thrower shouted from the back of the crowd. "Can I ring the bell, miss?"

Miss Jolly ignored him. "Howard," she said, "you can ring the bell until Johnny comes back. Come along in and I will show you where it's kept."

"Lucky thing," said one of the girls, who stood a little apart from the others and stared at him from black eyes under a pulled-down yellow woolly hat as How followed Miss Jolly into the school. Impulsively, he pulled off his glove to reveal the slip of stone on the palm of his hand. "I found this on the path, miss," he said. "Is it very old?"

Miss Jolly picked up the stone and peered at it through her glasses. "It is indeed," she said. "This is a neolithic arrowhead, Howard. This tapered end would fit into a stick, you see." Unexpectedly, she smiled at him as she returned the arrowhead. "Are you interested in old things?" she asked.

"Yes, sort of," said How. He thought it would seem rude to admit that the old things he really liked were secondhand salable items. He regretted having had to leave the bundle of fur scraps at home, but his mother had been firm about his taking nothing more than was necessary.

Miss Jolly handed him the heavy brass bell, and How said, "Thank you." He went on thinking about that last Sunday morning in London as he pushed his way out of the door again. He had gone to see Clifford, but he wasn't there. Jean said he'd gone train spotting. So he'd sold the tin soldiers to John Dwyer for a penny each. They'd have been worth more if he'd had time to paint them.

The door swung shut behind him and, standing on the step, How swung the bell to and fro, and its clanging rang out across the fens. Everyone charged across the yard to the cloakroom door, but the girl who had said, "Lucky thing," stayed where she was. She wore a black coat that looked as if it had belonged to a grown-up, for it was long enough to reach to her boots, and her hair escaped in untidy strands from under the yellow hat. "Let me try," she said, and reached out her hand for the bell.

"I've rung it enough," said How.

"Go on," said the girl. "Don't be stingy." Her eyes were as black and bright as a bird's, and How suddenly remembered the young crow he and Clifford had rescued from a cat, a couple of summers ago. Jean had fed it on bread and milk and kept it in a box, and it seemed all right for several days, then died. He handed the bell to the girl.

She glanced at him with a gleam of delight. Then, holding the heavy bell in both hands, she threw herself into ringing it, turning from side to side to swing the bell through a wide arc that seemed to pull at her thin arms until How fancied that a last, extra-wide sweep might carry her clean off her feet and she would hurtle away into the sky and disappear into the mist.

The door opened and Mr. Wicklow, who taught the seniors, came out. He was very thin, and his knuckles were red with chilblains. "Anna Rose, that is quite enough," he said. "You are not asked to ring the bell for *fun*." Then he frowned at How and added, "Why are you standing there, boy? You should be in the cloak-room with the others."

"But—" How began, then stopped. It would get the girl into trouble if he explained that Miss Jolly had asked him to ring the bell.

"Perhaps he could take it in for me," said the girl sweetly, and pushed the bell into How's hands. Then she was gone, running away toward the cloakroom door with a kicking up of black boots and a flash of yellow from the floppy knitted hat.

Mr. Wicklow stared after her disapprovingly. "I shall have to have a word with Miss Jolly," he said, and held out his knobby hand to How for the bell. How gave it to him, then followed the girl called Anna Rose across the misty yard.

Compared with How's school in London, the brown-varnished classroom was very crowded. The children sat in close-packed rows on the wooden benches. How supposed it was because of the evacuees. Stanley had said the London kids ought to have brought a teacher of their own with them and have had a separate school somewhere else. They did that in some of the other villages, he said, and it was better. "Vaccies" shouldn't come pushing into the village schools. And he had grinned, trying his best to be annoying.

How pulled his thoughts away from the irritating subject of Stanley. Miss Jolly was talking about history. "History is very exciting," she was saying. "Roger Bull, take that stupid grin off your face. It *is* exciting to discover that people lived in this very place, many hundreds of years ago. They were not pictures in books; they were real. They saw the same sky that we see and heard the birds sing, just as we do. And sometimes we are lucky enough to find something that they actually used." She glanced in How's direction, and his heart sank. She was going to ask him to show the class his arrowhead, and they would think he was showing off.

"Now, Howard has found something very interesting," Miss Jolly went on. "Come along, Howard, and show the class."

Reluctantly, How stood up. From the row behind him, Billy Thrower leaned forward and poked him in the back. *"Teacher's pet,"* he whispered. His voice was not loud enough to reach Miss Jolly, but How heard it. He wished he had left the beastly arrowhead where it was.

At playtime, a faint yellowish radiance was starting to shine through the misty sky, but it was still cold. Most of the boys charged about after a football, their breath steaming like cattle, and the girls chattered in groups or skipped or played clapping games. How watched, standing alone near the cloakroom door with his hands in his pockets.

The girl called Anna Rose came across the playground. "Can I look at your arrowhead?" she asked.

How fished the scrap of stone out of his pocket, grateful for someone to talk to.

"I wonder if it shot anyone," said Anna, turning the arrowhead over in her fingers.

"More likely a rabbit or something," said How.

"Poor little thing," said Anna. "I'd rather it was a person. Some people *need* shooting," she added fiercely.

How was startled. "Why?" he asked. "Oh, Germans, you mean, because of the war?"

Anna's face flushed suddenly. "Germans are all right," she said. "Most of them. No, just people, that's all. Animals don't ever do you any harm." Her black eyes stared into How's with an anger he did not understand. Then she dropped the arrowhead back into his hand and ran off, and How saw her trying to argue her way into a hopscotch game. He stared after her, moving aside absently as the football shot past his legs.

"Couldn't you have stopped it?" shouted Billy Thrower as one of the gang charged past How to kick the ball back. "Sissy!"

"I'm not a sissy!" How shouted back, suddenly annoyed.

"Yes, you are," said Billy. "Go and play with the girls."

24

"I can talk to who I like," said How, knowing this was a reference to Anna.

The boys grinned, glancing at each other. "You don't want to talk to *her*," said Roger. "They're foreigners. Her mother's a witch, too."

"Don't be stupid," said How. "There aren't any witches."

Billy hooted with laughter. "That's what you think," he said. "I tell you, she is. We all know."

Mr. Wicklow came out and rang the bell.

"You wait and see!" shouted Roger over his shoulder as they all ran in. "Billy's right. Foreigners aren't like us."

How followed them slowly. It was weird, he thought, to be warned against witchcraft and against people being foreign, as if it was all the same thing. Whatever sort of place *was* this?

Lessons in this school seemed to be mostly sitting still and listening, How thought, smothering a yawn. Perhaps it was because of the wartime shortages. There just weren't enough books to read or notebooks to write in. Or perhaps it was because Miss Jolly was so old-fashioned. She was talking about someone called Saint Gilbert, and the evacuees were giggling behind their hands because they thought it was a funny name.

Miss Jolly pounced on one of them. "Ethel Tarbuck, stand up," she said.

Ethel got to her feet, blushing. She was a small, round

girl with short brown hair held at one side by a couple of hairclips.

"You will stand there until the end of the lesson," said Miss Jolly severely. "And I hope nobody else is going to be stupid." She stared at them all, then went on with her story about Saint Gilbert, whose mother had dreamed, before he was born, that the moon had settled in her lap.

Weird, How thought again. He only half listened as Miss Jolly told them about the Priory that Saint Gilbert had built somewhere around here, and about its outlying granges. There was something very odd about this place, he thought. A land which used to be under the sea, where people still believed in witchcraft and a lady had sat with the moon in her lap.

Suddenly, Miss Jolly's eye was on him. "Howard Grainger, are you listening?" she demanded.

How came back to reality with a jolt. Trying to look intelligent, he thought frantically of the last word he had heard. Ethel Tarbuck was still standing up. "Please, what's a grange?" he asked.

"I did tell you, said Miss Jolly. "A grange is a small farm. But I am glad you have the sense to *ask*, Howard, when you don't understand something." She paused, then added, "Your name comes from that word, of course. A grainger was the manager of a grange. Perhaps that explains your interest in old things." And she smiled.

How's face turned pink. He liked the idea of being connected to people who had lived here in the past, but he wished she had not mentioned it in front of Billy and the others.

"Does anyone know the little church where Saint Gilbert's Priory used to be?" Miss Jolly inquired, and several hands went up. "Good," she said. "Then some of you can tell Howard where it is at lunchtime. He might like to go and see it. Elsie, give out the hymn books, please, it is time for singing practice. Ethel, you may sit down."

A van arrived at twelve o'clock with big metal containers of mashed potatoes and sausages and carrots, followed by pudding and custard, dished out in platefuls for the children to eat at their desks. Afterward, they went out to play again. The sun had come out now, bright in a hard blue sky.

A small crowd of boys approached How, backing him up against the wall near the toilets, under a thicket of ivy.

"You like old things," said Billy, grinning. He glanced at Harry Doggett and said, "He'd like the old house, wouldn't he, Harry?"

"Oh, he'd love that," Harry agreed.

How stared at them suspiciously.

"Sunday morning," Billy said to him. "You come up to the old house. We'll tell you how to get there."

"It's all tumbling down," Roger said enticingly. "Ever so old."

"No, thanks," said How.

"We're only being friendly," said Billy, prodding a

dirty forefinger into How's raincoat. "You want friends, don't you?"

How made no answer. He knew what invitations of that sort meant, and he did not want to go anywhere with Billy Thrower and his mob. Out of the corner of his eye, he caught a glimpse of yellow hat and realized that Anna was standing behind him.

"Shove off, you," Roger said to Anna. He returned his attention to How and added, "Eleven o'clock, Sunday. You'd better be there."

"He'd better not," said Anna fiercely. "And neither had you," she told Roger. "None of you. It's not your place. It doesn't like you."

"Ah, shut up," said Billy. "You're nuts, you are. Go on, shove off."

Anna stayed obstinately where she was, and Billy pushed her, hard. He was much bigger than she was, and she staggered back and almost fell, but she still did not go away.

"Your mother's a German, isn't she?" said Harry, narrow-eyed. "Germans eat all horrible things. Does she feed you frogs for breakfast?"

"She picks nettles to cook up instead of cabbage," Roger put in. "My dad's seen her. And she can't speak proper English. Just mumbo jumbo."

Anna's eyes filled with tears and she clenched her fists. "Just you shut up!" she shouted.

"Leave her alone," said How recklessly. "She's all right."

"Who says?" asked Harry.

"I do," said How.

"You're crazy," said Billy, and, with a sudden grab, he snatched Anna's yellow hat from her head and tossed it to Roger. Anna made a dive for it, but Roger threw it high in the air and it landed in a muddy corner of the playground, where several people who were playing a game of tag ran over it. All the boys dived after it but How got there first. He grabbed the hat and clutched it to his chest, and then Billy caught him. The others piled in behind him and, under their combined weight, How crashed to the ground. He managed to roll sideways as the boys battered at him, trying to pull Anna's hat out of his hands. He hunched himself into a ball, ducking his head to avoid their blows. He could taste blood in his mouth and knew he had cut his lip. Suddenly he heard a shout of "Hey! You boys, get off him!"

The boys peeled away, and How found himself being hauled to his feet by Stanley, watched with amusement by some of his friends from the seniors.

"You great twerp," said Stanley, brushing How down a bit with his hand. "What you playing at?"

Wordlessly, How handed the mud-spattered hat to Anna. She took it and walked away across the playground with her head bent.

"Just look at your coat," said Stanley. "Mum'll have something to say."

"I couldn't help it," muttered How. Gingerly, he wiped his mouth with the back of his hand and left a streak of blood. His knees hurt, too.

"You don't want to get mixed up with Anna Rose,"

Stanley warned. "She's bad luck, she is. You wouldn't know, being new here, but I'm telling you."

How wished people would stop telling him things, but he felt a bit shaky and, besides, he was grateful to his big cousin for rescuing him. So he just said, "Thanks, anyway."

Stanley gave a snort of fatherly contempt and said, "Kids." He and his friends strolled away across the playground, leaving How to inspect his grazed knees. They were not too bad, he thought.

One of the senior boys came out and rang the bell, and everyone ran in. Following the others, How looked over his shoulder and saw Anna, who was sitting very still on the end of the wooden bench in the middle of the playground, looking down at the yellow hat that she held her hands. How was reminded of the lady who sat in a dream with the moon in her lap. There was something terribly sad about it. "You all right?" he called.

Anna did not answer, but she got up and started across the playground toward the school.

In the crush at the cloakroom door, Billy Thrower said in How's ear, "I *dare* you, How Grainger. Be at the old house, Sunday morning. Eleven o'clock."

Dares could not be ignored. How turned his head and looked Billy in the eye. "Sunday morning it is," he said.

THREE

◆

All through the next lesson, the boys sitting behind How leaned forward to whisper instructions about the way to the old house, whenever Miss Jolly wasn't looking. Finally Billy passed him a blackly scrawled map on a piece of paper torn out of his math book.

But this time, Miss Jolly *was* looking. "Howard, bring me that," she said. She frowned at the scrap of paper, obviously not understanding what it meant. "Did you want to know the way somewhere?" she asked.

How had been thinking furiously. He dared not say anything about the old house. He could feel a silent menace coming from behind him. Keep quiet—*or else*. But he could not deny that the drawing was a map. Inspiration came. "I wanted to know where the church was," he said guiltily. "The one you were talking about—where Saint Gilbert was."

"Ah," said Miss Jolly. "I see. Yes, indeed." She returned Billy's map to How, with a last glance at it. "That isn't very clear," she said. "I think I had better draw you a better one. You may sit down—and thank you, Billy, for being helpful. That was very kind. But another time, be helpful *outside* the classroom, if you don't mind."

"Yes, miss," said Billy innocently. The other boys stared out of the window, trying not to giggle.

At the end of the afternoon, Miss Jolly gave How a very neat little map showing the exact location of the church. "If you go there, you can see the foundations of the Priory," she said, "and the Holy Well, where the monks came to get water."

"Thank you," said How.

"Not at all," said Miss Jolly. "I'm glad to see that you are taking an interest in your new surroundings." She smiled at him, and How turned pink. She was really quite nice, he thought. He felt bad about deceiving her. There was only one way to set it right. He would have to go and look at the church.

As usual, How walked home alone. Halfway along the field path, he was overtaken by a couple of children he recognized as evacuees, a boy and a girl. They ran past, then the girl turned, hopping on one foot, and called back to How, "You from Limehouse?"

"No," said How, imagining she meant a local village. "I'm from London."

"Limehouse is part of London, stupid," said the boy.

"Oh," said How, mentally kicking himself for his blunder. "Yes, of course. I'm from Catford."

"Eee-w," they both said, looking at each other, *"south* London. Posh."

How thought of the narrow streets of small terraced

houses and felt fiercely protective. "Don't you call it posh," he said. It wasn't stuck-up and expensive, like they thought. It was *home*.

"Garn," said the boy. "All south Londoners is posh."

"Even if you *are* all dirty," said the girl, pointing at How's coat, still muddy from the fight over Anna's hat. Then they ran on, laughing.

How stared after them resentfully. They were even worse than Billy Thrower, he thought. It wasn't *his* fault he hadn't been born in Limehouse.

When How arrived at Auntie's Kath's house, he hesitated outside the door and then went on to the yard at the back, hoping Uncle Jack would be there. The yard was empty, so he turned back. As he did so, a truck pulled in and stopped. How's uncle got out and said, "All right, are you?"

"Yes, thank you," said How. It was nice, he thought, that Uncle Jack hadn't mentioned the mud. A large young man in coveralls was getting out from the truck's other side. He seemed to be almost twice the size of Uncle Jack. His hair was short and brown, like an animal's fur, and his eyes were a clear, cornflower blue.

"That's Digger Bailey," said Uncle Jack, indicating the young man with a jerk of his head. "Been in the Army, but they couldn't do nothing with him. Sent him home after a bit."

The young man's eyes did not blink. "They got funny ways in the Army," he said slowly. "Wanted me to keep saying a number."

"Name and number, he means," said Uncle Jack. "I'll never forget mine. Eight-three-three-eight-six, Grainger, Sergeant. Royal Field Artillery. 'Course, that was in the last lot. They're on to eight-figure numbers now."

"They gave me a rifle," Digger went on. "Only they said I had to lie down. I couldn't fire it lying down."

"And he's been shooting rabbits since he was a kid," said Uncle Jack. "You had your tea yet, How?"

"No," said How. "I came to see if you were here. Look, I found this." He showed his uncle the arrowhead, and Digger came to look at it as well.

"I find things sometimes," Digger remarked. "I found a little man. Spading 'taters, I was. Just little." He held a dirty finger and thumb a few inches apart.

How stared at him, fascinated. Whatever did he mean? A toy soldier, perhaps.

"You could see him if you like," Digger offered. "I got a lot of things."

It sounded almost as good as a market stall, How thought. "Can I come tomorrow?" he asked eagerly. "It's a Saturday—I'll be home from school." Digger might have some bargains.

"Saturdays is football," said Digger thoughtfully. "I like football."

"Sunday, then," said How.

"Sunday be all right," Digger agreed, then said again, "I like football."

"Off you go home now, Digger," said Uncle Jack. "While it's light."

"All right," said Digger obediently. He retrieved a dilapidated bicycle that leaned against the barn wall, got on it, and pedaled carefully away.

"But I don't know where he lives!" said How, disappointed.

"I'll tell you how to get there," said Uncle Jack. "Him and his father live together, out along the fen. The old man keeps him in order. Used to be in the Navy, Ben Bailey did, before his wife died. Come on in and get your tea."

"Where've you been?" demanded Auntie Kath, fixing How with a fierce eye as he came in with Uncle Jack. "Stanley came in ages ago."

"Stanley's got a bike," How pointed out. "He gets here quicker than me."

"Never mind if he's got a bike or not," retorted Auntie Kath. "You've had time to be in this house twenty minutes or more. And just look at your coat."

"Sorry," said How.

"He was talking to me," said Uncle Jack.

Auntie Kath gave him a disparaging glance and said, "Huh!" She dumped a plate of scones down on the table and added, "Don't blame me if your tea's cold."

"I never have," said Uncle Jack, and went out to the kitchen to wash his hands. Water, How had discovered, came from the pump in the yard, which was used by the neighboring house as well. He went out to join his uncle. "Does Digger work for you?" he asked.

"Off and on," Uncle Jack said, pouring water into an enamel bowl from the jug that stood by the sink. "He does a bit on the farms, plowing time and harvest. That's when he finds most of his stuff, turned up behind the horses when he's plowing."

How put the block of red soap back on its dish and asked, "What have you been doing today?"

"Mending a roof," said Uncle Jack. "Then we been down at the station. I had a part load came in on a freight car. Digger helped unload it and stack it on the truck. Slates, mostly. You have to be careful with slates."

How dried his hands, thinking about the station. It seemed like the last connection with London, with its busy chuffings and whistlings and the smell of smoke. "I wish I could have seen Mum off," he said. "But I was at school."

"Ah, you mean Sleaford, on the main line," said Uncle Jack as they went back to where Auntie Kath and Stanley were sitting at the table. "The station you came to when I fetched you in the truck. No, Digger and I were just down the road in Billingborough. The branch line comes out here, you see. They shunt the freight cars into the sidings if there's goods to unload."

Clifford would be interested in that, How thought. He accepted a piece of cheese on toast from Auntie Kath and said, "Thank you. What do the freight cars carry?" he asked.

"Coal mostly," said Uncle Jack. "Vegetables in the summer. Sugar beets."

36

"Wool," put in Stanley.

How looked at him, puzzled. He had often held a skein of wool for his mother to wind into a ball, and it made his arms ache. But why did they carry it about in freight cars? "For knitting?" he asked.

"No, off the sheep," said Stanley with contempt. "The fleeces go up to Bradford for spinning. You don't know nothing, you don't." Then he added deliberately, "And you don't want to have anything to do with Billy Thrower and that lot. Nor with Anna Rose, neither." He glanced at his mother.

"Anna's all right," said How.

Auntie Kath paused in cutting a slice of bread. "Now, you listen to me," she said, tapping the table beside How's plate with the tip of the knife. "I won't say too much about the state your coat's in, being as you're a stranger here. Not this time. But I don't want you getting in any more fights, d'you hear me?"

"Yes," said How.

"And you don't want to get mixed up with those foreigners, either," his aunt added, slapping the completed slice of bread onto the plate with the others. "Mrs. Rose or whatever she calls herself. Most likely she changed it from what it used to be. They came from Germany." She tucked in her fat chins, sawing another slice off the loaf. "Keep themselves to themselves, they do, and I'm not surprised. From what I hear, they ought to be back there."

"Now, Kath, there's no proof of anything like that," Uncle Jack said mildly. "There's a lot of wild rumors, but you know what people are for gossip."

"They say Anna's mother's a witch," put in Stanley, nodding.

"I wouldn't go that far," said Auntie Kath. "But all the same," she added to How, "you leave well alone."

How swallowed his last mouthful of cheese on toast and licked his fingers, hoping his aunt would not notice that he had made no promises. Uncle Jack gave him the ghost of a wink.

The next morning was Saturday, and How didn't know what to do. He got out the letter from his mother that had arrived on Thursday and read it again.

"I hope you're getting on all right," it said, "and not missing the old Blitz too much, pardon my little joke. I've been going in Kitty's shelter across the road. It's only an Anderson, but I suppose they're all right, even if they are just corrugated iron, really. At least she hasn't got a dog—only a tortoise, and that's asleep for the winter. I hope your school is all right. I saw Clifford the other day and he said to say hello. I'll write every weekend when I've got a bit of time off from the factory, so you'll get a letter Tuesday or Wednesday and you'll know things are all right here. Give my love to Auntie Kath and Uncle Jack and Stanley. Love, Mum." And a row of *x*'s.

How had read the letter several times already, although it didn't really say anything. Saturday yawned ahead of him, dauntingly empty. Stanley had gone out on his bike with some friends. How found an old *Rupert*

Annual on the shelf of Auntie Kath's treadle sewing machine and sat down with it at the dining-room table, his elbows on the dark green plush cloth. Then Uncle Jack poked his head in and said, "You want to come into Bourne? I'm going to the auction sale."

"Oh, yes, please!" said How. His day had been transformed. "I'll go and get my coat."

His uncle nodded. "I'll start the truck," he said.

On the long, rattling ride across the fens to the town, How found himself telling Uncle Jack all about his interest in buying and selling things, and about Clifford's model railway, and about the market. His uncle nodded occasionally and at last said, "It'll seem a bit dull for you up here."

"A bit," How admitted. Then he added, "But I don't know the place yet."

"Right," said Uncle Jack.

The auction was hugely enjoyable. Furniture was stacked around the sides of the auction room, and the buyers sat on wooden benches in the middle. There were carpets and bedding and clothes as well, but the auctioneer began with what he called "outdoor effects"—hedging tools and harness and hay knives, timber and pantiles, two pony traps, a cement mixer, a lot of chicken coops, and a whole heap of stuff whose purpose How could not even guess at.

Uncle Jack bought the cement mixer and a complete window frame and several lengths of guttering and pipes, and bid unsuccessfully for some other lots of mixed stuff as well.

"Shame," said How sympathetically as the auctioneer's hammer came down in favor of someone else for the third time.

"Doesn't matter," said Uncle Jack. He raised a finger to a man on the other side of the hall and added, "I'll see him after. We'll fix it between us."

How was not sure what he meant, but he did not ask. The auctioneer started on the indoor stuff, beginning with saucepans and bundles of bed linen. Porters in green baize aprons held up each item as it was offered for sale. How was entranced. He must tell Clifford about this, he thought. There was an auction room near them in London, with gas stoves and washstands on view in its hallway, but he had never realized that they handled such a wealth of small stuff as well.

Uncle Jack bought a flower vase for Auntie Kath, and the next item was a bundle of mixed clothing, tied with string. Sticking out from the top was a red and white knitted scarf.

"Digger would like that," said Uncle Jack, nodding at the scarf. "He's got no mum to knit for him. And those are the colors of his football team."

The bidding stood at threepence. How shot his hand into the air. "Fourpence I'm bid," said the auctioneer, nodding in How's direction. "Any advance on fourpence?" He glanced around the room, then brought his hammer down. "Name?"

"Grainger," said How.

The auctioneer smiled and looked at Uncle Jack. "That all right, sir?" he asked, and How realized that he was assuming that How's purchases would go on his uncle's account.

"*Howard* Grainger," How said firmly, and everyone laughed.

"Do like the boy says," Uncle Jack instructed. He never seemed to smile, How thought.

During the course of the morning, How bought a box of assorted toys, a bundle of children's books, and a small bag containing what the auctioneer described as "sundry trinkets." The total cost was one shilling and eleven pence, as How had calculated, but when he went with his uncle to the office to pay his account, he discovered that there was a handling charge of twopence, which brought his bill to two shillings and a penny.

"I've only got two shillings!" he said in dismay.

"Here you are," said Uncle Jack, supplying a penny.

"Oh, *thank* you," said How.

"That's all right," said Uncle Jack. "You haven't had your pocket money yet, have you?"

"No," How agreed. "There's sixpence to come. Auntie Kath said she'd give it to me, because Mum left her some money, but she was busy this morning. I'll ask her when we get home."

But Uncle Jack was running his eye down his list of purchases and did not seem to be paying much attention. He handed How his own list and said, "Come on. We'll go and load up."

In the yard behind the auction rooms, How was intrigued to see that the goods his uncle had ended up with were rather different from the ones he had bought. Perhaps, he thought, it had something to do with his uncle's muttered conversations with various men during the sale. "What happened to the cement mixer?" he asked.

"Took a profit on it," said Uncle Jack. "Man I know got here late, missed it. I've got a cement mixer already, see, and he really wanted one. So I sold it on to him."

"For more than you paid for it," said How.

"Just a bit," said Uncle Jack. "Made ten bob. Would you like a sandwich?"

"Yes, please," said How. "And I owe you a penny."

Uncle Jack at last smiled. "Don't worry about that," he said.

Driving home across the flat landscape after a snack in a café, How felt happier than he had all week. It was late afternoon by now, and the sun was sinking toward the fen's edge like a glowing red tiddlywink. How told his uncle about the lady who dreamed about the moon. "She thought it meant her baby was going to be somebody wonderful," he said. "Do you believe in dreams?"

Uncle Jack hauled the wheel around to overtake a horse and cart plodding along the road, then he said, "You can choose, can't you. What you believe in, that's your own business."

"Yes," said How. "I suppose it is." In London, he thought, dreams had belonged to the nighttime, down in the stuffy shelter. Here, in some strange way, they seemed to be a part of everything.

Back at the yard, How helped his uncle unload the truck. All the stuff was hard and heavy, and he got a splinter in his hand from a length of timber. It was nearly dark by the time they went in through the back door to find Auntie Kath frying sausages. She looked at How's armful of purchases and said, "I hope you're not turning out to be a magpie like your uncle. At least he doesn't bring his stuff in the house."

"It'll be going out again," How assured her. "It's all for selling to other people."

Auntie Kath shot her husband a look and said, "Where have I heard *that* before?" Then she saw How's hands, dirty from handling tiles and fence posts and guttering, and added, "Don't you go upstairs like that." She noticed the splinter, too, and when he had washed his hands, she sat him down on a chair beside the oil lamp while she went to get a needle from her sewing basket. Getting the splinter out was a long and uncomfortable business, and How was glad to escape at last to his bedroom. Stanley was listening to a comedy program on the radio downstairs. The radio was the only electrical thing in the house, and it worked from a strange kind of battery called an accumulator, which Stanley or Uncle Jack sometimes took down to the garage for recharging.

By the light of the candle that burned in its china candlestick on the bedside table, How inspected his purchases. They looked promising, he thought. He undid the string from around the bundle of clothes and found that the scarf was wonderfully long and woolly. It had a couple of moth holes in it, but he didn't think Digger would mind that too much. With any luck, he would have something worth swapping it for.

The rest of the bundle was mostly old shirts, but there was a striped sweater that How thought he could wear himself, and a thin, silky blouse with flowers on it that his mother would like. Auntie Kath was too fat; otherwise, he might have given it to her. She had been pleased with Uncle Jack's vase. The shirts all had frayed collars and various missing buttons. He put them on the end of the bed as rejects. The books, too, were mixed. Some of them were the kind with pictures of girls with long hair standing among lilies, but there was *The Wonder Book of Living Things* as well, and *Boys' Own School Stories* and *Emil and the Detectives*. Better than the *Rupert Annual*. The toys were mostly rather paintless Dinky cars and Meccano bits, but they had possibilities.

The bag of "sundry trinkets" was made of black silk, with a slightly unraveling tracery of small black beads stitched across it. How opened the bag and tipped out the contents on the washstand. There was a tangle of necklaces and clips and brooches, some of them with empty sockets where the glass stones had come out, and How wondered if he had been rash in paying ninepence for it. One of the rings was quite pretty, with a biggish red stone surrounded by little white ones, but all the rings were much too big for the girls at school to wear.

The faint, stale breath of violets that came from the bag made him wrinkle his nose in distaste. Still, he told himself, girls always liked beads. He began to disentangle the necklaces, then heard Auntie Kath's voice from downstairs. "You want your tea, you best come and get it."

"Coming!" How shouted back. He was very hungry. He scooped the trinkets back into their bag and then, for safekeeping, lugged his suitcase out from under the bed and crammed all his purchases into it. Then, feeling that his life now had some purpose again, he picked up the shirts from the end of the bed, blew out the candle, and went downstairs.

FOUR

◆

The next morning, Sunday, How fetched Digger's scarf from upstairs, tucking it out of sight inside his coat. He didn't want a whole lot of questions from Stanley about what he was up to. It was none of his business.

"Lunch at half past twelve," said Auntie Kath as How let himself out of the back door. The kitchen was very steamy and smelled of boiling meat. "Don't be late, will you." She smiled at him. She had been very pleased with the shirts. The collars only wanted turning, she said, and with a new button here and there, they'd do fine for Jack, for work.

How promised not to be late. He shut the door carefully and walked down the path at the side of the house to the front gate. His uncle was in the garden, picking brussels sprouts, and he looked up when he saw How and said, "All right, are you?"

"Yes, thanks," said How. The instructions Uncle Jack had given him yesterday were clear in his mind. He knew where Digger Bailey lived—and he knew, too, that it was fairly near the old house. Things had worked out well. This way, he could keep the appointment with Billy Thrower at eleven o'clock without having to tell anyone where he was going. He set off down the road. It was a windy day, with clouds scudding across the sky, and the water sparkled in the deep dike beside the grass bank.

When he came to the track his uncle had told him about, How followed it across the fields with his shoulders hunched against the wind. His gas mask, slung as always in its cardboard box across his shoulder, caught the breeze and bumped against his back. It was never as windy as this in London, he thought. And never as muddy. The stuff clung to his boots in great lumps, and when he came to a deep puddle, he shuffled through it carefully, rubbing his boots together to try and clean them.

After a long walk, he came to a wider road, raised like a kind of causeway above the level of the fen. He crossed this, and went on a little farther. Then he saw a brick-built cottage standing at the edge of a village. The dike ran under a wooden bridge that led to its front gate, and a piebald pony looked over the fence from a small paddock behind a clutter of sheds, pricking its ears at the sight of How.

An old man was digging the garden in a very businesslike way, with a string stretched between two pegs on either side of the trench, to make sure it was straight. He looked up at How's approach and said, "You come to see the boy?"

How was not sure who he meant. "I wanted to see Digger," he said.

"That's it," said the old man. "He told me, Friday. But he's most likely forgotten by now. You'll find him in the shed, with his stuff. That first one, there." He pointed to the nearest of the outbuildings, a small wooden shed whose door stood ajar, then turned back to his trench.

"Thank you," said How.

Digger appeared at the shed door when How tapped on it. His face looked blank.

"I came to look at the things," How reminded him. "You said I could. At Uncle Jack's. Jack Grainger," he added.

"Oh . . . Mr. Grainger. That's right." A smile broke across Digger's face. "You come and look."

How followed him into the shed, leaving the door open for the sake of some daylight. Laid out on a corner of the bench by the shed's wall was a collection of what How recognized at once as junk. Most of it consisted of stones of all shapes and sizes, some of them, he saw, containing fossils.

Digger ran his hands over them affectionately. "I like them," he said. There were old bottles, thick and green and earthy, and pieces of curiously shaped tree root. There were several bones and pieces of pottery and metal, including something that looked as if it used to be a knife blade, and there was a pile of misshapen coins. Digger picked up a handful of these proudly and said, "Gold."

How didn't think they looked like gold, but he wasn't going to argue. Digger's collection was disappointing, he thought—hardly worth all that long walk. But you couldn't find a bargain every time. How lugged the scarf out of his coat, where it had lain bulkily against his chest.

"I brought you this," he said. "Uncle Jack says it's the colors of your football team."

Digger stared at the scarf without touching it. "For me?" he said.

"Yes," said How impatiently. "Go on—take it."

"Oh," breathed Digger. "That's nice. That's really nice." Clumsily, he wound the scarf around his neck. Then he beamed happily and gave a couple of small bounces like a toddler jumping for joy.

"Careful," said How. The shed was rather old, and it certainly didn't seem strong enough for someone of Digger's size to bounce in.

Digger rubbed the end of the scarf against his face. Then he went to the end of the bench and dug about in a cardboard box full of small stones and buttons and snail shells. "Here," he said, picking something out with finger and thumb. "You can have the little man. He'll like you. Bring you luck."

He gave How a small figure made of some kind of greenish black metal. It was, How thought, more like a boy than a little man, very slim, and clad only in a cloth wrapped around the hips and reaching to the ankles. It had the feeling of something very old, and yet it was finely detailed, leaning forward slightly from its feet, arms extended. One hand was missing. There was a strange eagerness about it.

How felt a flutter of excitement as he looked at the small figure lying in his hand. It was something very special—and he couldn't take it. It was too good. "You can't give me this," he said. "Not just for a scarf."

Digger did not understand. His face fell. "Can't I keep the scarf?" he asked.

"Of course you can keep the scarf," How assured him. "But you ought to keep the little man as well."

Digger smiled again. "Dolls and things," he said. "I'm too big. You have him." And he added again, "Bring you luck."

The old man appeared at the doorway of the shed. "Just look at *you*," he said, nodding at Digger with the scarf wound around his neck. "Where'd you get that?"

"He give it me," said Digger, indicating How.

"And Digger's given me this," said How. He showed the old man the little figure and went on, "Only I don't think he should. It might be really valuable."

The old man glanced at the figure without much interest and said, "Not to him it i'n't. Money don't matter, boy. It's what you like as matters. If he thinks he's had a good bargain, then he has. And I should know—I'm his father." He hung up his spade and garden line on a couple of nails in the shed wall.

"It's one thing less to clutter up my shed, anyway," he said. "I wish he'd find somewhere else to keep his rubbish." He went out, then, struck by another thought, looked back to add, "Digger, you can peel some spuds for lunch when you got a minute."

"All right," said Digger.

How thought it could not be anywhere near lunch-time. But it might be getting near eleven o'clock. "I must go," he said. "Thank you very much for the little man. I'll take great care of him."

Digger nodded. "Reckon you will," he said.

How went back along the road the way he had come. Billy Thrower's crumpled map was in his pocket, along with Miss Jolly's neat one, under the small, cool weight of the little figure. If it was really going to bring him luck as Digger had said, How thought, then it had better start doing it now. Butterflies of fear fluttered in his stomach at the thought of Billy and the others, waiting for him in the old house.

A clump of trees stood dark against the sky, with a winding, weedy track leading across the fields to the house that lay hidden in the wood. How turned off the road onto this track and followed it up the gently rising ground toward the trees. There were bushes and un-kempt hedges on either side of him, and the track nar-rowed to no more than a muddy slit between the grass-covered ridges that had once been a drive.

How trudged on, wondering if he had found the right place. The boys couldn't have come this way; otherwise the grass would show some sign of being flattened by people walking over it. Then, ahead of him, he saw a pair of tall, rusted iron gates set about by overgrown laurel bushes. How looked at the gates with a tinge of disapproval. In London, he thought, all the park gates and railings had been taken away at the beginning of the war, to be melted down and turned into guns. He stopped and stared at these. They were so deeply buried in a tangle of blackberry branches and the long, brown strands of last year's grass that he couldn't see a way to get near them. And, in any case, they were fastened by a heavy, rusted chain and a large padlock. Behind them, the old house stood quietly amid the tangle of its jungly garden. Some of its windows had glass still in them, but others were black and empty, so that it looked as if it was dozing with an eye half-open.

With a flicker of hope, How wondered if the boys had lost interest in the dare and simply not turned up. Then he heard a sound which killed that idea stone dead. Though faint, it came clearly from the half-hidden house. It was a hoot of laughter that could come from only one person—Billy Thrower. So they were in there, waiting for him.

How plunged back to the path again, following it on around the side of the house, with the bramble-smothered railings on his right. "Cross by the tree," the boys had said, among a confusing mass of instructions—but what tree? In this wood, there were hundreds of them. And there was no gap in the railings. There seemed to be no way into the house. How went on, ducking under hawthorn bushes and fending off the long branches of elder that blocked his way.

Then, ahead of him, he saw that the path was completely blocked by the huge bulk of a fallen tree. Its roots stuck up into the air on How's left, where they had been torn out of the earth when it had blown down, and its top end had come crashing down across the iron railings on his right, squashing them flat. Perhaps, he thought, he could climb over the flattened railings— but, even as he thought it, he saw that they were too deeply buried in prickly brambles. The tree must have fallen a long time ago. He would simply have to climb over it and look for a gap on the other side.

The tree was such a fat one that How could not see over it, but he managed to scramble up. He found that its top surface was covered with mud, and when he cautiously got to his feet, feeling as if he was balancing on the back of an enormous wooden horse, he understood why. On the far side of the tree, the thicket gave way to a plowed field with a muddy path along the edge of it. And the path led straight to the tree's root end. People had come this way often and climbed up to where How was standing now, with their feet muddy from the field. How thumped himself on the forehead in sudden understanding. Of course! "Cross by the tree." This is what the boys had meant.

Balancing carefully, he made his way along the slippery trunk and jumped down on the far side of the flattened railings into the tangled garden. A trodden pathway through the grass and weeds ran ahead of him to a door in the side of the house that stood, as Digger's shed door had done, slightly ajar. But, unlike the dark little shed, this doorway seemed to glow with a faint light. How prickled with caution as he picked his way toward it along the path. There was no sound of laughter now; the silence hummed in How's ears, and he knew they were aware of his presence. Most probably, from some upstairs window, they had been watching him ever since he had come to the front gates.

He reached the door and paused, with his hand on the rusted latch. Then he took a deep breath, pushed the door open hard, and stepped inside.

His heart almost stopped with terror.

The room in which he found himself was filled with a flickering radiance. And it came from the glowing eyes in a dark head, from which sprouted long, curving horns. Ivy grew so thickly across the broken windows that hardly any daylight came in.

How gave a breathless gasp, and someone who had been standing behind the door was suddenly close behind and put his hand over How's eyes. How jabbed backward with his elbow, hard, and heard whoever it was grunt with pain, but someone else grabbed him around the neck. In the next instant, he was in a full-scale fight. He did not know how many of them there were, but when Billy Thrower's face was momentarily in front of him, he hit it on the nose and saw it instantly spout with blood.

There was no hope of winning. Their sheer weight overwhelmed him and someone kicked him behind his knees, so that his legs doubled up and he collapsed on the rubble-strewn brick floor with several boys on top of him.

"All right," said Billy. "That'll do. Get up," he added to How. They hauled him to his feet. Panting, and with his fists clenched, he glared at them.

"He's a good fighter," Harry Doggett remarked.

"Fair," admitted Billy, and mopped his nose on the turned-back sleeve of his jacket. Roger Bull was there as well, How saw, and a ratty-haired boy called Eric Figg. He glanced again at the terrifying head with the glowing eyes and, now that he was used to the dim light, he saw that it was nothing but the skull of a horned sheep, standing on top of the old brick oven and lit from behind by a candle.

"Scared you, didn't it?" said Roger, grinning.

"Not really," said How. He hoped he sounded brave.

"You haven't done the scary bit yet," said Billy. "Come on."

The other boys grabbed How by the arms, and Billy led the way out of the room to a hall where a broad staircase went up in front of them. They bundled How up these stairs to a half-landing where the stairs turned and went up again, arriving on a much larger landing with bedroom doors opening off it, directly above the hall they had come from. Here, several of the banisters edging the landing had broken, leaving a gap large enough to fall through. How hoped that Billy's scary bit had nothing to do with that gap, for they all seemed to be looking at it.

His hope was in vain. Billy stood by the banisters and said, "Come here." How did as he was told, and Billy pointed through the gap and said, "See that bar?"

How nodded. The iron bar was a little below him, about six feet away. It ran from the wall on his left, above the stairwell, to the banister rail on his right, halfway down that flight of stairs. It looked as if it had been put there to hold the banisters up, he thought. Or the wall. He wondered if the house was more crumbly than it looked.

"This is the darc," said Billy. "You stand at the gap and jump through it. Catch that bar with your hands. From there, you can swing down to the landing where the stairs turn around. Like Tarzan."

"If you miss it," put in Eric Figg gleefully, "you'll fall all the way down."

"I can see that, you idiot," said How. The sight of the drop below the bar was sickening. The gray flagstones of the hall below looked a horribly long way down. He looked at Billy. "Have you done it?" he asked.

"Dozens of times," said Billy. His light brown eyes did not leave How's. "I bet you won't," he said. The others stood a little behind him, watching.

How started to undo the buttons of his raincoat. His fingers felt clumsy. "I can't jump in this," he said. He seemed to be living in a dream. There were dreams everywhere in this place, a part of his mind observed, and he remembered being in the truck with Uncle Jack. He wished he was there again, where it was rattly and safe and real. He folded his raincoat carefully and laid it beside his gas mask on the worm-eaten floorboards, feeling the weight of the little figure in its pocket as he did so.

"You best take your boots off as well," said Harry. "If you're really going to do it. We didn't think you would."

How said nothing. Treading on the heel of first one boot and then the other, he pulled his feet out of them. As usually happened, his boots managed to keep his socks inside them, in a little heap at the toes. How fished the socks out and shook them, then decided against putting them on again. He draped them over the edge of the boots. Then, wiping his palms against the sides of his shorts, he walked to the gap in the banisters and crouched there, with his fingers on the floor's edge.

He knew that if he looked down, he couldn't do it. He stared fixedly at the bar. If the others could reach it, so could he. They knew the bar wouldn't break. It wouldn't come away from the wall and let him go crashing down to the stone floor of the hall below. He held his hands out like a diver. His bare toes were wriggling, trying to find a good grip on the dusty floorboards.

"Don't be stupid," said Roger Bull suddenly. "You can't do it. You don't have to." His voice sounded scared.

"Shut up," said Billy tersely. "I want to see him do it."

The bar could be reached, How told himself. It *could*.

He jumped.

The bar was under his chest, almost at waist level. He had jumped too hard. He was going to tip forward and fall face first. He clung on desperately, fighting for his balance.

"Now the landing," said Billy excitedly. "Go on, you can do it."

How knew he had to do the next bit quickly, before the panic that hammered in his chest overcame him completely. This was not like Tarzan, who made it all look so easy. Very carefully, he took a firm grip of the bar with both hands. It pressed hard into the front of his sweater as he leaned across it. The awful bit was going to be when he had to let himself down to hang at arms' length.

He eased himself back from the bar. The jerk of his own weight seemed as if it would pull his arms out of their sockets. Then he knew he was all right. The worst part was over. Hanging from his hands, he took a deep, shuddering breath and, for the first time, looked ahead of him to the half-landing. He was filled with a sudden elation. It was not too far away. He could do it. He swung his knees forward and back a couple of times, then, on a forward swing, let go, and the grimy floorboards were there to catch him.

He stood up and dusted his hands nonchalantly. Then he turned and walked up the stairs to where the group of boys were smiling uneasily. None of them said anything. How sat down and put his socks on. He enjoyed the feel of their gray woolliness. He enjoyed breathing. He might have been down there on the hall floor with a broken leg, or worse. He stepped into his boots and put on his coat while they watched him. He

58

picked up his gas mask. "I'll have to go," he said. "I promised I wouldn't be late for lunch."

They nodded. Then Billy said, "Show you the way across the fields if you like. It's quicker than coming through the wood like you did." His face looked a terrible mess, smeared with drying blood.

"Thanks," said How. As he and Billy went down the stairs, with the others following behind, he glanced up at the iron bar. There was now, he saw, a distinct dip in it.

FIVE

❖

"Oh, my goodness," said Auntie Kath as How came into the kitchen. "Just look at your eye. Who did that to you?"

How was vaguely aware that his left eye hurt rather a lot, and it seemed to be closing up, but he had been too concerned about getting home in time for lunch to worry about it.

"Quite a shiner you've got there," said Uncle Jack, sharpening a carving knife. "Have you got sore knuckles as well?"

"Yes," said How.

"I've told you before, I won't have you fighting," Auntie Kath scolded. "Where have you been? You're absolutely filthy."

"I know where he's been," said Stanley. "Billy Thrower and that lot were trying to get him to go to the old house. I heard them. That's where he's been."

"Is that right, Howard?" demanded Auntie Kath.

How nodded.

Her face turned bright red. "If you were my boy, I'd

put you over my knee and tan your backside, that I would," she said. "Going about with rough boys like that. Those Throwers, they're horse dealers. Got plenty of money, yet they choose to go about looking like tramps. And getting into fights and ruining your clothes—what would your mother say?" Not waiting for an answer, she rushed on, "Somebody else's child, it's a big responsibility. It's not like one of your own. What am I going to tell her if you get into bad company?"

She took a large saucepan of potatoes off the top of the stove and drained it into the sink, and the cloud of steam made her face even redder. "And with this blessed war on," she added, "I can't even get a bit of steak to put on your eye."

Uncle Jack tested the knife on his thumb and put the steel back in the drawer. "The thing is," he said to How, "old houses can be dangerous. Rotten floorboards and stairs—you could fall through and hurt yourself."

How almost smiled. "Yes," he said. "I suppose I could."

"Don't you ever go there again," said Auntie Kath, pounding at the potatoes in the saucepan with a thick wooden tool she called a stumper. "Or I'll be really cross. You hear me?"

"Yes," said How again.

Lunch was boiled ribs of mutton with brussels sprouts and the mashed potatoes, followed by jam tart and custard. Auntie Kath, who seemed to have recovered her temper, served huge quantities of everything and tutted when How couldn't finish it up. "No wonder you're such a skinny rabbit," she said.

Stanley reached across for How's plate and started spooning up what he had left. "That's why you get whapped, fighting," he said. "Not big enough."

How thought of Billy Thrower's nose, but decided not to say anything. Uncle Jack glanced at him and said dryly, "I'd like to see the other feller." But Auntie Kath had gone into the kitchen with a pile of dishes and did not hear.

Sunday afternoon promised to be dull. Uncle Jack settled in his chair for a snooze and Stanley reluctantly got his homework books out, while Auntie Kath sat down with a cup of tea at her elbow and a pile of socks to darn.

"I think I might go and look at the little church," How ventured. "Miss Jolly was talking about it. She gave me a map to show the way."

Auntie Kath squinted sideways at her needle as she threaded it. "Don't know what's the matter with you Londoners," she said. "Always running about. Never keep still long enough to get any flesh on your bones. Don't you go getting into any fights, mind."

"I won't," How promised.

"And keep away from that old house. And mind you're back here before dark!"

"All right," said How. As he went to get his coat and gas mask from the peg by the kitchen door, he felt very virtuous. This time, he was going to an approved-of place that had been suggested by his teacher, and he had no plans to meet anybody or to do anything alarming.

Another long walk lay ahead of him. Clifford would never believe this, he thought as he set out. Miles of muddy countryside, just to look at a church! Then a wave of homesickness swept over him at the memory of Clifford and the market and the friendly streets and pavements and garbage cans and the boarded-up shops with layers and layers of posters stuck on them. It was all cozy and close, not like this windswept place.

How shook his head, pushing the thought away. There was no sense in making himself miserable. One day, the war would be over and everything would go back to what the grown-ups called "normal," though How could hardly remember it. There would be lights on at night, and no air raids, and lots of things to buy in the shops. They wouldn't need ration books. And Dad would come home.

How did not often think about his father. He had seen him so seldom in the last four years that the soldier who came home on leave sometimes, to hug How's mother and sit in the kitchen talking to her endlessly, seemed to be just a special kind of visitor. And yet, How thought, having someone around like Uncle Jack would be really nice. Someone who got on with his own business, but was always there to talk to. Perhaps, he realized with some surprise, his father *was* like Uncle Jack. After all, they were brothers.

Occupied with these thoughts, How covered quite a lot of ground without noticing it and found himself at the narrow lane which, according to Miss Jolly's map, led across the fields to the church. The ground rose slightly here, and he could see a clump of trees against the skyline, with the spiky tower of the little church sticking up among them. Saint Gilbert had sense, How thought, building his Priory up there. It might not be quite so muddy on the higher ground.

The lane crossed a deep dike, turned at right angles, and continued up the gentle hill. As How neared the church he saw bicycles, a couple of cars, and a pony and trap parked in a clearing among the trees. He had not expected other people to be here—somehow, he had thought of the church purely as an ancient monument. But now he realized that a service must be in progress, and halted irresolutely. His parents were not church-goers, and How felt as if religion was something of a mystery. They had prayers at school, of course, and he enjoyed singing hymns. At the school in the village there was a picture of Jesus holding a lamb, in a frame with crisscross corners, and it gave How a wistful feeling, wishing he could be sure that someone *did* look after everything. But he wasn't sure. The jagged lumps of shrapnel rusting in their box in the kitchen at home belonged to a different world from the beautiful land-scape of the Good Shepherd. He went on slowly toward the church. Having come so far, it was silly to turn back now.

He went through the gate into the churchyard and walked quietly along the grass at the edge of the path. A voice rose and fell from inside the tall windows, and

How did not want his feet to make a noise on the gravel. Gravestones stood among the grass, and there was a line of trees parallel to the wall of the church. Between them, How saw, there were big pieces of broken masonry, some of them carved as if they had been part of an arch or a column. There was stone at his feet, too, great slabs of it. Walking slowly from slab to slab, How could see that they came from a large building, far bigger than the little church. And it was all gone.

Something Miss Jolly had read to them came back into his mind. "How are the mighty fallen, and the weapons of war perished." Only they weren't perished, How thought. They were flying about in the sky, dropping bombs on people. It was Gilbert's nice big Priory that had gone. It seemed the wrong way around, somehow.

The churchyard was on two levels, the lower one lying farther away from the church, down a shallow flight of brick steps where a small notice said "To the Holy Well." Oh, good, How thought. Miss Jolly had mentioned that. He looked along the path where the notice pointed—and stopped dead. A figure in black was sitting on the low wall at the edge of the grass, motionless, its back to him.

For a moment, How almost turned and ran. Was it a ghost? A monk who had lived in the old Priory? Common sense came to his rescue. Monks wore habits tied with rope around the waist, and they shaved the middle of their heads or wore a hood. The person who sat at the end of the path had a thick mass of dark hair. Cautiously, he made his way along the path toward it, but he gave a little gasp of alarm as the figure turned its head. And then he knew who it was. "Anna!" he said.

"I've been waiting," said Anna calmly. "I knew you'd come."

Huddled in her black coat as she perched on the low wall, she looked, How thought again, like a young crow.

"You should have worn your yellow hat," he said. "Then I'd have known it was you."

"My mother had to wash it," said Anna.

How nodded, remembering the scuffle in the playground. He stared at the Holy Well. He expected it to be a thing like the pictures in the nursery rhyme books, with a little roof and a handle at the side to wind the buckets up and down, but he found himself looking into a spring of water just below the surface on which he stood, rising to fill a round hole between the stones, from which it ran away down a channel leading out through the hedge. The sun had disappeared behind a bank of heavy cloud and the brown fields were desolate. How gave a little shiver. Then he looked at Anna curiously. "What d'you mean, you knew I'd come?" he asked.

Anna gave a slight shrug. "I just did," she said. "I wanted to say thank you for sticking up for me." She glanced at him and added, "You've got a black eye."

"Yes," said How.

"That was the boys this morning, I suppose," said Anna. "I know they were at the house. Was it awful?"

"It could have been worse," said How, and he found himself telling her all about it.

"I expect they'll want you to be one of the gang now," Anna said when he came to the end. "I mean, you've passed their silly test."

How thought about it. "I don't mind Billy," he said, "in a way. But I don't go in for gangs. And that Eric Figg is a sniveling little twerp."

Anna smiled, and then there was a pause. "We could be friends," she ventured. "You don't have any friends here, and neither do I."

How remembered what Auntie Kath had said about Anna and her mother coming from Germany and wondered if it was true. "But you've lived here for ages, haven't you?" he said. "You know everyone."

Anna looked up at him darkly. "Knowing isn't being friends," she said, and the wind ruffled her black hair like feathers.

How smiled down at her. For someone so small, she was amazingly grown-up. "All right," he said. "We'll be friends." A spatter of rain broke from the dark clouds.

Anna jumped to her feet, her face alight with excitement. "We must drink to it!" she said. "That's what people do when there's something to celebrate."

She knelt by the circle of stones where the clear water welled up and reached down to dip her hand in it, holding the sleeve of her black coat back with the other hand. She raised a dripping palmful and, with her eyes on How, said, "I am your friend. Always." She sipped the water, then let the rest trickle through her fingers. "Now you do it," she said.

How knelt and dipped his hand in the water. It was icy cold. "I am your friend," he repeated. "Always." And he drank.

As if in celebration, the organ pealed out suddenly from the church. "We must go!" said Anna, scrambling up. She did not wait for How, but grabbed up her gas mask and ran down the path between the gravestones and out of the gate.

"Wait!" called How. He set off after her, but she did not slacken her pace until she was well clear of the grove of trees, nearly halfway down the track that led to the road. Then she stopped and let How catch up with her. The organ sounded distant now, but its music still rang clearly across the fen.

"What's the matter?" asked How.

"They'll be coming out in a minute," said Anna, with a fearful glance over her shoulder. How frowned, puzzled, and she went on, "I don't want them to see me. People think I'm bad luck. Haven't they told you?"

"That's all rubbish," said How stoutly. But, in his raincoat pocket, his fingers curled around the little figure that Digger had given him. "Bring you luck," Digger had said. And it had worked for him in the old house. Everyone needed luck. How thought of that last night at home, when they had slept downstairs in the dining room. "Keep our fingers crossed," his mother had said.

He walked on beside Anna in the falling rain. A car and a couple of bicycles overtook them, and the rain suddenly increased in intensity. A flash of lightning cracked across the sky, followed by a rumble of thunder.

Anna broke into a run. "This way!" she shouted back to How, and turned off the track, plunging into a narrow, overgrown path.

"Where are you going?" How called after her. Trees on either side of the path almost met overhead and the long stalks of dead grass leaned together in front of him, dripping their burden of water across his legs as he pushed through them, so that it trickled down the inside of his boots. He stumbled on. The rain was creeping down his neck from his saturated hair, finding its way inside his raincoat collar. His socks were soaked. This was crazy, he thought.

Then, ahead of him, he saw Anna duck down to squeeze through a gap in an iron fence and run on toward a tall house, dark against the gray sky. For a moment, he stopped. Oh, no, he thought. Not again. He had not realized that they were coming to the old house. This was a different entrance to it, perhaps one which only Anna knew. And she was running, not toward the house itself, but to a smaller building with a curiously arched roof and a door that sagged half-open from its hinges. She disappeared inside.

How, following, found himself in a cobwebbed stable. Worm-eaten wooden pegs stuck out from the walls with stiffening harness hanging from them, and a semicircular iron hayrack was mounted at the end of a roomy stall, with a deep wooden manger below it. Anna, scattering drops of water from her hair and her coat, was scrambling up from the manger to the hayrack.

"What are you doing?" panted How.

"You'll see," said Anna. She clambered up onto the hayrack like a monkey and crouched there, reaching up to a trap door in the roof and pushing the wooden cover aside. As she stood upright on the hayrack's edge, her head and shoulders disappeared into the loft and, with a wriggle, she hitched herself up into it and was gone from sight. Her face reappeared in the open rectangle of the trap door. "Come on up," she said.

In his waterlogged coat and boots, How found it difficult, but he managed it after a struggle and arrived on his hands and knees on the dusty floor of the hayloft. A window high up in the wall let in a shaft of grayish daylight and, although the rain rattled on the roof, the loft was warm and dry. There was a pile of hay stacked almost to the roof in one corner. Anna had sat down on a wooden box, watching him. Beside her, a plank on a couple of bricks acted as a table, on which was a tin mug, a tall enamel jug with water in it, and an apple. Another box was covered by a fringed, embroidered shawl, and on this stood a jar with a bunch of snowdrops in it, together with several books and a rag doll.

Anna was looking serious. "You've got to promise you won't tell *anyone* you came here," she said. "This place is secret. Nobody else in the world knows about it, not even my mother. This is the kitchen," she added, indicating the plank table, "and that's the lounge." She pointed to the shawl-covered box.

"It's wonderful," said How. "You're lucky Billy and the gang have never found it."

Anna got up and went to the trap door, where she replaced the wooden cover. Then she slid a flat steel bar into place across it, slipping it under iron loops on either side. "You see?" she said. "It locks. They came into the stable once when I was here, and they climbed up and tried the door, but I'd locked it. And they never tried again—I suppose they think it can't be opened."

"Lucky," said How. "Because you can't lock it when you're out, can you?"

"Oh, no," said Anna. She went across to the pile of hay and climbed up it until she could just see out of the little window, then beckoned to How to join her. "Look," she said. "You can see down to the garden. So I always know if someone's coming across here from the house. And over there"—she pointed, peering sideways—"where that little thatched roof is, among the trees, that's our cottage."

"On the other side of the field?" said How, with his face against the dusty glass.

"That's right," said Anna. She slid down the heap of hay. "There's no road to it or anything. But there's a path across the field."

How followed her back to the makeshift table and sat down on the floor.

"Does your eye hurt?" asked Anna after a pause.

"A bit," said How.

She hugged her knees with her arms, frowning. "I

hate them coming here," she said. "Billy and that lot. It's such a nice house, and it doesn't like them being here. I know it doesn't." She looked up at How and added, "I came here early this morning. I thought of something to try to frighten them off, but it didn't work."

"The sheep's skull?" asked How.

Anna nodded. "They're always going on about my mother being a witch and rubbish like that," she said, "so I thought, if I did something a bit witchy, they might think it was real and run away. But they weren't scared."

"I expect they were when they first saw it," said How. "I was. Only they'd had time to get used to it." He laughed, and asked, "Where on earth did you get it?"

"From Digger Bailey," said Anna.

"Digger? Oh, I know him!" said How, and felt, for the first time, a faint sense of belonging to this strange place he had come to. He fished in the pocket of his wet raincoat. "Look—he gave me this, in exchange for a football scarf."

Anna took the small figure carefully. In silence, she held it upright on the palm of her hand, and they both gazed at it. "I think it's an angel," she said.

"Angels have wings," How objected. "And long white robes and halos."

"That's only the way people draw them," said Anna. "They don't *know*, do they? This is an angel all right— look at the way he's holding his arms out, as if he's protecting us."

"Digger said it would bring luck," said How.

"*He*," corrected Anna. "Not it. Yes. I think he will." She stood the angel carefully in front of the little pot of snowdrops.

"That's a good place for him," said How. "There's nowhere to keep him at Auntie Kath's, only in my pockets, or else in my suitcase under the bed."

Anna hugged her knees again, with her thin wrists sticking out of her wet black coat. "I'd like to make this place really beautiful," she said. "Full of flowers and lovely things."

How thought. "I've got some strings of beads and stuff," he said. "Trinkets. There's a nice necklace you can have for here. I'll sell the rest to the girls at school."

"That would be lovely," said Anna. After a pause, she added, "Why do you want to sell things?"

"Because it's interesting," said How. "If you sell one thing, you can buy something else. Things keep changing."

Anna nodded and tucked a strand of wet black hair back from her face. "I see," she said. "I thought you meant you were saving up for something."

"Not really," said How. And yet, even as he said it, he realized that he wanted to gather some money together. Not for anything special—but just in case.

Six

◆

It was some time before the rain eased off enough to go out, and when How arrived back at Auntie Kath's house, the daylight was fading. But, he thought, nobody could call it dark. He wasn't late.

Stanley was circling his bike in the puddled road outside the house, and he grinned when he saw How.

"You'll catch it," he said.

"Why?" asked How. "I said I'd be back before dark, and I am."

"You been talking to that girl Anna Rose," said Stanley. "Johnny Parfitt saw you, on the road down from the church. He passed you on his bike."

"And you told Auntie Kath, I suppose," said How bitterly.

"No, I never," said Stanley, shaking his head. "Didn't have to. Johnny's mother came in to see if Mum had a spool of thread she could lend her. She told her."

How could imagine. The women in the village seemed to spend a lot of time talking. He had seen them, standing outside the shop with their heads together.

When he walked past, he felt that they stopped talking and watched him.

Stanley circled the bike again, then came to a halt beside How with a grating of gravel as he put his foot down. "Listen," he said. "I told you—you don't want to be seen about with her. I'm not being funny, honest." His fat face was creased and earnest. "You've only just come here, so you don't know. They're weird, her and her mother. They're bad luck. And you can *catch* bad luck, like measles."

How said nothing. It was a ridiculous idea, but Stanley was not being nasty. He was really trying to give How some good advice. But it seemed crazy. Anna was all right. She was just lonely, that was all. People had given her a bad time. And in any case, How could not let her down now. He had dipped his hand in the water and promised to be her friend. He went into the house.

Auntie Kath pounced on him at once. "Where have you been?" she demanded.

"Up to the little church, like I said," How told her.

"And where else?" asked Auntie Kath. "You were walking down the lane with Anna Rose. Where did you go?"

How didn't know what to say. He could not tell his aunt about the hayloft. It was Anna's special place, her secret hideaway. And it was his, too. The angel stood on guard in front of the jar of snowdrops.

"Come on," his aunt insisted. "I want to know where you've been."

"Just walking about," said How vaguely.

"In all that pouring rain?" Auntie Kath snorted. "A likely story."

"Well, we sheltered for a bit," How admitted.

"Where?"

How shrugged. "It was a sort of barn," he said, and added appealingly, "My feet are ever so wet."

To his relief, Auntie Kath began to fuss about his wet clothes, and he hoped she had forgotten her questions. "Get those boots off," she instructed. "I'll stuff them with newspaper. Put some dry socks on, and hang your coat by the fire. You townies, you've got no sense at all. Any boy of mine would at least know where he'd been. But I don't want to hear any more about you keeping company with that girl, you hear me?"

"Yes," said How uneasily.

At school the next day, Billy and the others had their heads together in the corner of the yard, and How wondered what they were up to. They looked at him as he walked past, and Billy raised a hand in greeting, but none of them said anything.

How went across to talk to Anna as she came in through the gate, but, to his surprise, she ran past him to push her way into a line of girls who were jumping over a long skipping rope turned by two of them. Later, in the jostling crowd at the cloakroom door, she said in his ear, "Best you aren't seen about with me." And she had moved away before he could say anything.

After morning prayers, Billy put his hand up and said, "Miss, do you believe in devils?"

"The Devil walks amongst us all the time," said Miss Jolly severely.

"Yes," said Billy, "but have you ever seen one?"

Miss Jolly frowned at him. "Of course not," she said. "Nobody has."

"We have!" said Billy, and his friends nodded in agreement. "In the old house, all lit up. Someone's been doing something wicked. Playing at witches or something."

The girls gasped and looked round-eyed, and heads turned to look at Anna, who sat as still as stone, staring at the blackboard, on which nothing had yet been written.

Miss Jolly started to say something, but, almost to his own surprise, How heard his own voice say loudly, "It was just an old sheep's skull with a candle behind it."

Billy and the others glared at him, and Anna darted him a glance which was half gratitude and half fear.

"None of you should be in the old house at all," said Miss Jolly firmly. "And there should certainly be no playing about with candles. I'm sure I don't need to remind you that we are at war. We are lucky here not to see much enemy activity, but you know perfectly well that any light showing at night could be seen by an enemy aircraft. Whatever you have been up to, it sounds extremely foolish, and you are *not* to do it again. Susan, give out the math books, please."

And that was that.

■ ■ ■

At playtime, the boys surrounded How, and Billy said, "Why didn't you shut up?"

"Why didn't *you?*" How retorted. "You were only trying to make trouble."

"*We* didn't put the candle there," Billy told him. "Or the skull. They were there when we arrived."

How knew that, but he tried to look surprised.

"You heard what Anna said about not liking us going there," said Harry. "And they say her mother does weird sorts of things. It must have been her. *And* they're foreigners."

"We blew the candle out when we came out of the house," Roger added virtuously. "But what if we hadn't? It might have still been burning when it got dark."

Anna would have blown it out when she came down from the hayloft, How thought—but he could not say so.

"I tell you, she's bad luck," said Billy. "We *know.*"

"You *think* you know," corrected How, and he walked off across the playground with his hands in his pockets. He wished they would all mind their own business.

When How went home that afternoon, he found Uncle Jack sitting in his chair by the fire with his right arm swathed in bandages, his hand held across his chest by a sling. He looked up as How came in and said, as usual, "All right, are you?"

"Yes," said How, staring anxiously, "but what about you?"

Auntie Kath came out of the kitchen, drying her hands, and said, "Broken his collarbone."

"It wasn't my fault," said Uncle Jack, as if he had been accused of carelessness. "A tread of the ladder broke. I went right through it."

Stanley looked up from his perusal of one of the books How had bought and said, "Bad luck, isn't it. Told you." And his eyes met How's in triumph.

"Could happen to anyone," said Uncle Jack. "Nuisance, though. I can't drive the truck or anything."

How took his coat off and hung it up. He felt oddly uneasy.

Auntie Kath pursed her lips and said, "*And* I dropped one of my best cups this morning. Drat," she added, and dived back into the kitchen, from which came the sound of hissing milk and the smell of burning.

That wasn't the end of it. The next day, How sold a Dinky car to an evacuee boy called Len, and that very afternoon, Len was sent home with a raging toothache. Janice Warnock gave How two colored pencils as a swap for a brooch and got a black mark from Miss Jolly for poking bits of blotting paper into an inkwell, and Beryl Fish tore her dress in a game of French He just after she'd given How twopence for a locket on a ribbon.

"Told you," said Stanley again, as Miss Jolly led the weeping Beryl into the school to mend her dress with a safety pin.

Anna stood by the wall alone, her hands stuffed into the sleeves of her black coat like a monk as she gazed across the fen, and when How went across to speak to her she turned her head away and said, "Don't. It'll only cause more trouble." Then she glanced back at him and added, "Saturday morning. In the secret place." And walked away.

Later that week, Auntie Kath left her purse on the bus when she was coming back from Bourne, and Stanley, cycling behind a sugar beet truck, skidded on a patch of mud and landed in the dike with a buckled front wheel.

And there was no letter from How's mother. She had said she would write each weekend. How scanned the single letter he had received from her, though he knew every word by heart. He had answered it straight away, dropping his letter into the postbox in the village last Thursday. That was a week ago. For the first time, he wished his house had a telephone. It had never seemed to matter before. He mentioned his worries to Auntie Kath, who was bad-temperedly chopping wood outside the back door—a job Uncle Jack always did before his accident—and she said, "I expect she's busy. You'll just have to be patient."

Friday came and went, and there was still no letter. Uncle Jack sat morosely in front of the fire with his arm wrapped in the white triangle of the sling, listening to the radio. How perched on the chair beside him and said, "I'm sorry about your arm."

"Blasted nuisance," said Uncle Jack glumly.

After a pause, How asked, "Do you think it was bad luck? I mean, like they say?" Knowing that Auntie Kath was listening from the kitchen, he dared not mention Anna's name. He had given her a blue necklace for the loft hideaway in the playground at break, and Stanley had seen him and shaken his head.

" 'Course not," said Uncle Jack. "That's a lot of nonsense. The ladder was rotten. I shouldn't have been using it, but new ones are hard to come by these days."

Auntie Kath came in with a bowl of potatoes to peel, turning the velour cover back and putting a newspaper on the table's wooden surface before she set the bowl on it. "Luck or no luck," she said to How, "while you're in my care, I'll want to know what sort of company you're keeping. And it's not to be Anna Rose."

Uncle Jack reached forward with his good hand and turned the radio up. "May as well hear the news," he said.

How listened dutifully, though he never understood why grown-ups were so keen on the news. It was all about places he had never heard of, where the war was happening outside Britain, with phrases like "counter-offensive" and "tactical withdrawal." The home news always came last. To the rasp of Auntie Kath's knife as she set about the potatoes, the announcer said, "There has been slight enemy activity over southern England. Several enemy aircraft are reported to have been shot down."

Slight enemy activity. That meant there had been a bad raid, How thought. He remembered a morning when they had stumbled up from the air-raid shelter to find most of the windows in the house broken and tiles lying all over the garden from its roof, whose rafters stood open to the sky. Everything smelled of earth and cordite, and when they went into the house the floor crunched underfoot because of the plaster that had been shaken down from the ceilings. Only a brown trickle of water had come from the tap, and the electricity was off. So was the gas. They had come on again by lunchtime, and when How's mother had switched on the radio, the announcer had used the same phrase as the one How had just heard. "Slight enemy activity over southern England."

How went upstairs and sat on the big, lumpy, double bed he shared with Stanley. "Keep our fingers crossed," his mother had said. He crossed the fingers of both hands and looked at them, then spread them out again and pressed his hands on his knees, trying to subdue the ache of anxiety he felt inside him. Crossing fingers was not enough. "Please, God," he whispered. "Please." He was not sure what he was asking for, but it was something, and it was very important.

The next morning was a Saturday again, and there was still no letter from How's mother. How had woken early, and he watched the post-lady ride past the gate on her bicycle without stopping, then sat down dejectedly on the edge of the bed. The linoleum was chilly under his bare feet but he did not want to get back under the blankets beside Stanley, who was still asleep.

Shivering, he pulled his clothes on and crept downstairs. The curtains were still drawn, and their wooden rings rattled on their rail as he pulled them back a little. The fire was no more than gray ash behind its screen, and the room was very cold.

How went across the frosty yard to the outside toilet, then came back to the kitchen. When he picked up the jug of water that stood by the sink, he found that a thin layer of ice lay across its surface. He poked his finger through it and poured some water into the tin basin, dabbled his hands in it half-heartedly, and wiped his face on the towel. Then he got the loaf out of the enamel breadbin with BREAD lettered on its lid and cut off a slice. He knew Auntie Kath kept the butter ration in the meat safe and thought he had better not take any in case it was more than his share. He spread some plum jam on his bread and ate it.

He still felt hungry, but he thought Auntie Kath would not like him helping himself to things. He fidgeted aimlessly for a while, then put his raincoat on. Perhaps the shop in the village would be open by now. They might have some chocolate. He felt carefully in his inside pocket for the strip of paper squares called Personal Points that entitled him to his ration of sweets, then let himself quietly out of the back door. He walked around the side of the house and down the garden path where the knobbly brussels sprouts stalks stood almost as tall as he was, and started down the lane toward the village.

The blind inside the shop door ran up as How approached it, the wooden acorn on the end of its cord swinging to and fro. He pushed the door open and went inside.

A gray-haired woman looked out from behind a stack of newspapers on the counter and said, "Yes?"

"Have you got any chocolate?" asked How.

"No," she said, with a lift of her chin.

How stared at her doubtfully. Usually, he thought, people said they were sorry when they hadn't got something. He felt faintly annoyed.

"Well, go along," said the woman.

How put on his most pathetic expression. "Isn't there just one little bar?" he asked. Trying to be even sadder, he added, "My uncle's got his arm in a sling. He's broken his shoulder."

"Oh," said the woman thoughtfully. "Are you Kath Grainger's nephew, then?"

"Yes," said How.

She bent down behind the counter and reappeared with two small bars of chocolate, one milk and one whole-nut. "You should have said," she told him. "We don't get enough for all these evacuees, you see. I've tried to get more, and they keep saying they'll put the quotas up, but they never do. Fivepence, please. Got your coupons?"

How pocketed the penny change from his sixpenny bit and checked his strip of coupons when she returned them, to make sure she hadn't cut off too many. Then he picked up his bars of chocolate and went out.

"Put those in your pocket!" the woman called after him. "And don't you go telling everyone I let you have them!"

"I won't," How assured her. Did she think he was born yesterday? He had learned in London to keep his mouth shut if anyone did him a favor. It was a pity about the whole-nut, he thought; he didn't like nuts much. But anything was better than nothing. He broke off two squares of milk chocolate and put them both in his mouth together and walked slowly back along the village street. The chocolate tasted wonderful.

The village clock struck eight. At home, How thought, he wouldn't have dreamed of getting up at this hour on a Saturday morning. The pleasure of the chocolate began to wear off. The post-lady pedaled slowly back along the street with her empty sack bundled in the carrier of her bike, and How wondered again why there had been no letter from his mother. Anxiety made his stomach feel tight, and the thought of sitting about in Auntie Kath's cold house with its ashy fire and darkened rooms was very unattractive. When How reached the cottage he found himself walking straight past it, with a furtive glance at the windows to see if anyone was looking out.

Without really meaning to, he went on walking until he came to the path across the fields that Billy had shown him. The grass along its edge was still white under the trees on his left, though the sun was well up now, melting the frost where it slanted across the clods of plowed earth. How came to the fallen tree and made his way carefully across its slippery surface, jumping down into the garden. He went in through the back door of the house and glanced at the ram's skull. It was much less sinister now, standing harmlessly in front of the burned-out stub of candle.

How walked across the room to the hall, where he paused to look up at the slightly bowed iron bar that crossed the stairwell above his head. He smiled faintly and walked on. Now he had the house to himself, he wanted to see more of it. He went from room to room staring curiously at the high ceilings with their molded edges, the elaborately tiled fireplaces, and tall French windows that must once have opened onto a sweep of lawn, though they were crisscrossed now by the long unpruned growths of honeysuckle and wisteria.

The house, How discovered, was L-shaped, one arm of it ending in a kitchen where a glass-fronted rack of bells stood high on the wall above a big iron range, each bell with a label under it—Master Bedroom, Morning Room, Study. He supposed that the bells rang to summon servants with cocoa or more coal for the fires. The other wing of the house ended in a cluster of two or three small rooms, but these were slightly different. Somehow, they suggested a place where cricket stumps and a bat would be thrown down on a summer afternoon, and the shallow stone sink under the window might be where a girl with a white apron over her long skirt had arranged flowers in a vase, delphiniums and tiger lilies and tall white daisies.

From this room a door led out to a paved yard. How tugged at the rusty bolt and hauled it open. Weeds grew between the flagstones, but there was an air of great peace about the place. It was contained on two sides by the walls of the house, which stood at right angles to each other, and a little distance away stood the stable block onto which How and Anna had dived in the pouring rain last Sunday.

How looked up at the little window, high in the apex of the gable, wondering if Anna was there, watching him. He walked across the courtyard and over the sun-thawed grass that grew in the gravel and went into the stable. There, he climbed up from manger to hayrack and pushed at the trap door. It rose easily on his hands, and he felt a slight disappointment. Anna could not be there—or had she left the door unfastened for him to get in?

He gazed around the loft, but it was empty. A shaft of early sunlight coming through the little window touched some yellow aconites that Anna had put in the jar in place of the snowdrops. The necklace How had given her lay in a carefully arranged circle around the feet of the angel on the shawl-covered box, like an offering, he thought. He sat down and waited. After all, it was still very early. He got the opened bar of milk chocolate out of his pocket and ate another square. After a while, he climbed up the sliding pile of hay and looked out of the window at the quiet, jungly garden that lay below, and stared across to the path leading to the half-hidden cottage. There was no sign of Anna.

How sat down on the hay. It smelled sweet, like a ghost of last year's summer. Imagining the sun hot in the sky above him, How lay back and put his wrist across his eyes. In another few minutes, he was fast asleep.

SEVEN

❖

"H ello."

The voice was close to his face. How opened his eyes, then turned his head away from the shaft of light that came from above him. The hayloft, he remembered. Of course.

"I'm glad you're here," said Anna. "I brought some bread. Would you like some?"

How sat up and yawned. Then the anxiety came back, worse than before, like a dull pain that had been waiting for him while he slept. He put his head in his hands.

"What's the matter?" asked Anna.

For a moment, How could not talk about it. Anna broke off half the hunk of bread she had taken from a paper bag and held it out to him. He took it, but did not eat any. "There should have been a letter from my mum," he said.

Anna looked at him consideringly. Then she said, "Couldn't you get your aunt to ring up?"

"She doesn't have a phone," said How. "Neither does Mum."

There was a pause. Anna nibbled a small piece of the dark bread. Then she said, "Do you think something's really happened?"

"I don't know," said How wretchedly. "I just feel awful, all the time. If something's happened, why doesn't somebody *say*?"

"Perhaps they can't," Anna pointed out. "Perhaps nobody knows your address."

"The Ogdens wouldn't know it," How agreed, more to himself than to Anna, then explained, "We had an argument with them about fleas in the shelter." Anna did not laugh, and he went on, "Mum said she was sleeping in Mrs. Armstrong's shelter across the road. Kitty, she calls her. But I don't know if Mum would have given her Auntie Kath's address."

"What about your dad?" asked Anna.

"He's away in the Army," said How. He did not want to think about what might have happened, but his fear would not leave him alone. "If Mum *can't* write to me," he said steadily, "then maybe nobody knows where I am." It was a very unsettling thought.

"Isn't there somebody *you* can write to?" asked Anna.

"I could write to Clifford," said How. If only he'd seen him on that last Sunday morning, he'd have given him Auntie Kath's address, he thought, and then shrugged. At that time, he hadn't known Auntie Kath's address himself. "But if I wrote to him today," he went on, "the letter wouldn't get there until Tuesday. Maybe longer, if it gets held up. And he might not write back straight away. He's only interested in railways, really. And I want to know what's *happened*."

"Then you'll have to go and find out," said Anna calmly. She laughed at his startled expression. "People here are so funny," she said. "They never seem to travel about. My mother and I have been to lots of places."

"Have you?" said How curiously.

Anna's smile faded. "Oh, yes," she said.

"Stanley said you came from Germany," said How, and added quickly, "but that's all right."

"Most people think it's all wrong," said Anna. "Even though we're British citizens now. It's called being naturalized. My mother changed her name and everything."

"When did you come here?" asked How.

"Before the war," said Anna. "My father had been arrested because he didn't agree with the Nazis. I can't remember him, really—I was quite small then. He never came back, then my mother heard that he was dead. We were traveling for a long time, and then we stayed with Aunt Elise in France. But the war had started, and when the Germans invaded France we had to move again."

"So you came here?" said How.

Anna shook her head. "Not straight away," she said. "We were in Southampton, but we got bombed out from there. But my mother had made friends with some people who owned this cottage, and they said we could rent it from them." She shrugged. "So here we are."

"Oh!" said How. "I thought you'd lived here for ages."

"No, only three years," said Anna. "That's why they still think of us as strangers. But traveling's all right. I mean, it's quite easy. You just—go."

"It costs money," said How practically, trying to subdue the leap of excitement he felt at the idea. "I don't know if I've got enough." He fished in his pocket and produced a handful of coins. "There should be four and sevenpence," he said. "I've sold quite a lot of things this week. I had four and eight, but I repaid Uncle Jack a penny I owed him."

They counted the money and found that How was right. "Is that enough for a train ticket?" asked Anna.

"I don't know," said How. "It doesn't seem much. I'll have to ask at the station at Sleaford. But I've got to *get* to Sleaford first. When Mum and I came, Uncle Jack met us with the truck."

"You can't tell them you're going?" said Anna, and it wasn't really a question.

How shook his head. "Auntie Kath would never let me," he said. After a pause, he added, "I'd like to tell Uncle Jack. But he's around the house all the time since he had that accident, and Auntie Kath's always there. And he's sort of grumpy, anyway."

"I expect his shoulder hurts," said Anna.

"It's more because he isn't working, I think," said How. "If you don't work, you don't earn any money."

Anna nodded. She got up from the pile of hay and went over to the plank table where How had left the half-eaten packet of milk chocolate. "Ooh, lovely!" she said, picking it up. "Can I have a bit?"

"Yes, of course," said How.

They shared the rest of the bar. Although How was feeling nervous about the plan that had arrived so suddenly, it was a tremendous relief to be able to share his nagging worry with someone else. And it was very pleasant, eating chocolate in the warm, hay-scented loft. Then he thought of something.

"Oh, heck," he said. "What's the time?"

"I don't know," said Anna. "About eleven, I suppose."

How jumped up. "They'll be wondering where I am," he said. "I didn't mean to go to sleep." He made for the trap door.

"Wait!" said Anna. She picked up the little figure from its place on the table. "You must take the angel," she said. "If you're really going to travel to London, you'll need the luck more than I do."

How slipped the angel into his pocket, and his eyes met Anna's. "Thanks," he said. "It's better than crossing fingers."

"Much better," said Anna.

How slid the cover back from the trap door and climbed down, feeling with his foot for the hayrack's edge. "Are you staying here?" he asked.

Anna, crouched above him, nodded. "For a bit," she said. "I'll think about you. It'll be all right. I'm sure it will."

"Yes," said How bravely. "Of course it will."

Outside, he turned to stare up at the little window. He waved, and thought he saw a hand wave back, but the sun was reflecting so brightly from the glass that he couldn't be sure.

How was nearing Auntie Kath's house when a bicycle skidded to a halt beside him. He looked around, expecting to see Stanley, but it was Billy Thrower, untidier than ever in an unraveling sweater and his jacket with the turned-back sleeves.

"Everyone's looking for you," said Billy. "Your aunt's in a terrible state."

"Oh, no," said How.

"Oh, yes," said Billy with relish. "You're really going to get it. Where've you been, anyway?"

"I just went down to the shop," said How evasively. "I fancied some chocolate."

Billy snorted. "She wouldn't give *you* any chocolate," he said. "You're an evacuee."

"Well, she did, so there," said How, forgetting his promise to keep quiet about it.

"Go on—bet she didn't," said Billy.

"What's this, then?" retorted How, hauling the bar of whole-nut out of his pocket. "Tell you what," he added, "I'll sell it to you if you like. Twopence-halfpenny."

Billy was not a horse trader's son for nothing. "Twopence," he said. "It's secondhand."

How put the bar of chocolate back in his pocket and turned away. "Bet you've used up all your coupons," he said.

"Oh, all right," said Billy. "Twopence-halfpenny." He fished a handful of money out of his pocket. There was quite a lot of it, How saw. And he needed money, badly. With a flash of inspiration, he said, "You can buy my sweet coupons if you like. I've got nearly a whole month's."

Billy eyed him speculatively. "How much?" he asked.

"Half a crown," said How promptly.

"Two bob," said Billy.

"Split the difference," said How. "Two and threepence."

"Done," said Billy, and he slapped How's palm as a sign that the bargain had been struck. "That's two and fivepence halfpenny I owe you, then, for the chocolate and the coupons." He poked among his handful of coins. "I haven't got a halfpenny."

"Give us half a crown, then, and I'll owe you a halfpenny," said How. "Till next week." He almost added, When I get back from London.

Billy was already biting the end off the bar of whole-nut. "Okay," he said, and handed How the silver coin.

How slipped it into his pocket and said, "I must go." The thought of Auntie Kath waiting for him was alarming.

"Okay," said Billy again. "Shall I tell her I've seen you?"

"Could do," said How. "It might make her feel a bit better."

"You'll be lucky," said Billy, and rode off.

This time, How was not lucky. He did not even find out whether Billy had delivered his message or not.

"Just what d'you think you're up to?" Auntie Kath shouted at him. "Sneaking out of the house like that—didn't even take your gas mask. I've just about had enough of you. Where've you been?"

How hung his head and said nothing.

"Come on," insisted Auntie Kath. "I want to know."

"You might as well tell her," Stanley advised.

Uncle Jack, in his chair by the fire, looked up from his newspaper and met How's eyes, then looked away again without smiling.

"I went down to the shop," said How. "I only meant to be a minute."

"At eight o'clock this morning, yes, Mrs. Biggs told me," said Auntie Kath. "More than four hours ago. Where have you been since then?"

How shook his head. He could not tell her.

"You've been talking to that Anna Rose again, haven't you?" demanded Auntie Kath. "Or else you've been poking about in the old house again. Which is it?"

Both, How thought guiltily. There was nothing he could say.

"You're a very naughty boy," said Auntie Kath. "Disobedient and sneaky and obstinate. Get upstairs. You're not coming down until I say so. And don't expect any pocket money from me, even if your mother did leave me some. Just wait until I tell her what you've been up to."

"*She'd* understand," said How, and he suddenly had the awful feeling that he was going to cry. He turned and bolted up the stairway behind its cupboard door to the privacy of the bedroom.

"And stay there!" Auntie Kath shouted after him.

How flung himself on the bed and wept. She shouldn't talk about his mother like that. Didn't she understand what might have happened?

After a while, How sat up and blew his nose. He could hear voices raised in the kitchen, where Auntie Kath and Uncle Jack seemed to be having an argument, but he couldn't hear the words. The sun was shining, and he went to the window and looked out. The fields lay calm and flat. Traveling is quite easy, Anna had said. You just go. How's unhappiness began to turn into a tough determination. He left the window and lugged his suitcase out from under the bed. He couldn't take it with him, obviously—it was too heavy, and it would attract too much attention. But there were some things he would need.

Auntie Kath's heavy footsteps sounded on the stairs, and How quickly pushed the case back. He was sitting dejectedly on the chair beside the bed when she came in with a plate of food and a knife and fork.

"Sausage pie," she announced, dumping the plate down on the washstand. "You can eat it up here. I'll send Stanley up with your dessert."

"Thank you," said How meekly.

"And don't be cheeky!" said Auntie Kath.

When she had gone, How ate some of the sausage pie, thinking hard. It was not going to be easy to get out of the house. Auntie Kath was nearly always lurking about downstairs and, since his accident, so was Uncle Jack. How felt sad about Uncle Jack. He would have liked to tell him about his plans, but the unsmiling look he had received this morning warned him not to. The staircase led straight down into the living room, so that was no good. He would have to get out some other way.

How glanced again at the window as he ate a bit of dark green cabbage, but he already knew that there was a sheer drop below it to the doorstep of the never-used front door. The only hope was the back of the house. The sloping roof of the kitchen was a lean-to, much lower than the rest of the house.

Stanley came up with a plate of custard. "You done it now," he said. "Why didn't you tell her where you'd been?"

"Couldn't," said How.

"Why not?" asked Stanley. "Here, can I finish your pie if you don't want it?" he added.

"You're welcome," said How.

"Where *did* you go, then?" asked Stanley through a mouthful.

"That's my business," said How.

Stanley shrugged. "Daft, you are," he said.

When How had eaten as much as he could of the

custard, Stanley finished that as well, then took the plates downstairs.

How thought carefully. After a while, he went to the top of the stairs and called down, "Auntie Kath, can I go to the toilet?"

"Yes," she said. "But you come straight back." She was doing the ironing in the living room as How walked through, with one flatiron clamped in her meaty hand while the other was heating on its grid over the fire, and she looked at him fiercely.

Outside, How surveyed the house carefully as he came out of the little shed. The kitchen roof, he saw, sloped down from just below the window of the back bedroom. And at the side of the house, there was a big willow tree that looked as if it was not too difficult to climb. Beyond that, Uncle Jack's yard backed onto the open fields.

How went back into the house. In the narrow corridor by the kitchen door, he felt in the pockets of his raincoat that hung there, retrieving the little figure of the angel. He wrapped it in a handkerchief and transferred it to the pocket of his shorts, then went back into the living room.

"Excuse me," he said, "but could I have some paper to write on?"

Uncle Jack said kindly, "Want to write a letter to your mum, do you?" He got up from his chair and, with his good hand, took a pad of lined paper from the drawer. "Got a pencil?" he asked.

"Yes, thank you," said How.

"And we'll have no telling tales," said Auntie Kath, looking up red-faced from her ironing. "You're being punished for disobedience, young man. And for being obstinate. When I ask a question, I want it answered."

"I'm not going to tell tales," said How. He went upstairs, and there he sat down on the bed with the pad of paper and wrote carefully:

Dear Aunty Cath and Uncle Jack, I had to go to London to see if Mum is all right. I couldent tell you. I am very sorry if you are woried but I will be all right.

Love, Howard.

He tore his letter off the pad and propped it against the tiled back of the washstand where it could easily be seen. Then he tore a few blank pages out of the pad, folded them carefully and put them in his pocket with the stub of pencil. Somehow, they seemed sensible things to take. He replaced the pad in front of his letter, then got his suitcase out again.

He wished now that he had made a bigger effort to sell everything he possibly could at school last week—but with Billy's half a crown from this morning, he had seven shillings and a penny. That wasn't too bad. He fished out the beaded black silk bag, which he had not tried to sell at school for fear that it would attract too much attention from Billy and the others. It was going to look very odd, he thought, but it was the only small bag he had. Quickly, he packed into it the few remaining Dinky toys and Meccano bits for Clifford, then dropped in the prettiest of the rings. He had wanted sixpence for it, but none of the girls would pay that much. He rolled up the flowered silky blouse very small and stuffed that in as well. Last of all he put in the angel. He couldn't take pajamas or anything—they were too bulky.

He stood frowning for a moment. There was no hope of getting his coat from downstairs, but he would need something warm. He was already wearing his school sweater, but he thought of the striped one he had bought with the bundle of clothes that had contained Digger's scarf. He hauled it out of the case and pulled it over his head. It was huge, he found. He had to roll the sleeves back several times, like Billy with his overlarge jacket, but it was very thick and warm.

How sat down on the bed to try and think carefully in case he had forgotten something important, but the butterflies in his stomach made it difficult to think at all. He closed the suitcase and pushed it back under the bed, then took a deep, shuddering breath. This was it.

EIGHT

❖

With a last look back at the note he had left on
the washstand, How picked up the beaded silk
bag and his gas mask and crept into the adjoining bedroom. He had never seen inside it before. A pair of
Auntie Kath's stockings hung over the brass bedrail,
and he felt horribly like a burglar. He tiptoed across
the rose-patterned carpet and, inch by inch, pushed the
window open. From downstairs, he could hear the
sound of a brass band coming from the radio. Good,
he thought. The music would help to mask any noise.
He put his head out of the window and looked down,
to find that the sloping roof was only just below the
windowsill.

How climbed out and carefully shut the window behind him. The angle of the roof seemed alarmingly steep
now that he was on it, and he felt scared of losing his
footing and slithering all the way down it. He worked
his way sideways, on hands and feet like a crab, impeded
a bit by his gas mask and the bag. He knew he was
above the kitchen, and expected at any moment to hear
Auntie Kath's voice from the yard below him. "And

just what d'you think *you're* doing?" she would ask. It was an awful thought. He reached the willow tree, whose branches leaned across the roof, and had to push his way through a mass of twigs that broke noisily. Even if she did hear him, How thought, he wasn't going back now. He would dodge her and run.

He crashed recklessly through the twigs and reached a strong branch, managed to get a foot over it, and scrambled down. The rough bark scraped the insides of his bare legs below the level of his gray flannel shorts as he eased his way down the tree, but at last he was on the ground. He crept away from the house until he gained the shelter of the barn wall, then fled across the yard.

He did not stop running until he was two fields away. Then, with his shoes covered in mud, he slowed to a walk. His heart was pounding in his chest and he felt very hot in his double layer of sweaters. He had planned to get to the railway station, but he wasn't sure where it was, and he dared not walk down the road to the village in case somebody saw him and immediately alerted Auntie Kath. He crossed another field, climbed a gate, and found himself in a narrow lane. He paused, wondering which way to go, then shrank back against the gate as he heard the rhythmic creaking of a bicycle approaching.

The cyclist came into sight around the bend, a large figure whose knees stuck out sideways as he pedaled. His neck was muffled in a red and white scarf.

"Digger!" said How.

The bicycle stopped with a high-pitched squeal of brakes, and Digger stared at him blankly. Then a smile of recognition broke across his face. "You're the boy who got the little man!" he said.

"That's right," said How. "I'm taking great care of him."

Digger nodded happily. "Bring you luck," he said again.

How hoped he was right. But there was something more important to ask him. "Digger," he said, "do you know the way to the station? The one at Billingborough?"

Digger nodded again. "I'm going to football," he said.

"Yes," said How patiently, "but I want to know where the station is."

"You can come on my bike," said Digger, indicating the crossbar.

"To the station?" asked How.

"Station's right near the football," said Digger.

It was not a comfortable ride, but How was grateful for it. The distance was farther than he had expected, and the lift had saved him a lot of time. "Thank you very much," he said as he got off the bicycle stiffly.

Digger smiled. Then he noticed the beaded bag that How had tucked under his arm. "That's pretty," he said.

"Yes," said How. He would give it to Digger, he thought, when he came back—if he still had it. "Don't be late for the football match," he added.

"Football," said Digger, forgetting about the bag. "Oh, yes. I like football."

"Bye-bye," said How.

"Bye-bye," Digger repeated obediently. Then he got on his bicycle and pedaled off.

There seemed to be nobody about in the station, which was very small, and How wondered where he could get a ticket. He walked through the little hall to the platform and found a man painting a white line along its edge. The man looked up, brush in hand, when he saw How, and grinned. "Government orders," he explained. "All platforms got to have white edges so passengers don't fall on the tracks in the blackout. Never mind if there aren't any passengers—orders is orders."

"Why aren't there any passengers?" asked How.

"Been no passengers on this line for ten years or more," said the man. "Goods only, this is." He surveyed How, looking at his oversized stripy sweater and his mud-plastered shoes. "You one of the evacuees?"

How nodded. No passengers. He was dumbfounded. What on earth was he to do now?

"Thought you must be," said the man. "Local kids know it's goods only. Train spotter, are you?"

It was a good explanation for his presence here, How realized. "That's right," he said, and he pulled the folded sheets of paper from his pocket, together with the stub of pencil. Clifford always carried a small notebook with him for writing down engine numbers, but the paper would have to do.

"A lot of the London kids are keen on that," said the

man. He looked at his watch. "Next train along is the two-forty-three for Sleaford. 'Course, that's a big station, Sleaford is. You can get to Spalding from there, or Grantham. London, even."

How nodded, trying to look casual, and the man went on painting.

How wandered slowly up the platform to stand at its end as he had seen Clifford do, peering intently up the line for the first sight of the train. Questions were raging in his mind. Was there any other way to start his journey to London apart from the train? There could be a bus to Sleaford, but he didn't want to walk into the middle of Billingborough and start asking people about buses. Everyone seemed to know each other here, and it was quite possible that whoever he asked might be a friend of Auntie Kath's. And grown-ups were terribly good at preventing you from doing things.

No, it would have to be the train, How decided. But would it stop at the station? And even if it did, would he be able to get on it? Uncle Jack had said the freight cars carried coal and vegetables and wool. In his imagination, How thought of tumbling into a carload of woolly fleeces. That would be a lovely way to go to Sleaford.

Then he began to think more realistically about what he was planning to do. If the train *did* stop, he would have to climb into a car, and it might be quite a scramble. He would need both hands free. His gas mask was not too bad, because its string went across his shoulders, but the beaded bag was going to be a nuisance. He frowned at it. Then he had an idea. He dumped everything on the platform and, crouching down, opened the gas mask box and unfolded the top of the rubber mask, whose oval mica window had to lie flat in case it cracked. He crammed the beaded bag and its contents inside the mask, pushing it down hard. Then he refolded the straps and eyepiece over it. The cardboard lid would hardly shut over the bulge, but at least he had his hands free.

How stood up and slung the mask over his shoulder again, stuffing the bits of paper into his pocket. His heart was beating very fast.

A small plume of smoke appeared in the distance. The train was coming. Suddenly How realized that it was going to be almost impossible to get on to the train without being seen. He glanced back at the man, who had painted his way up the platform to the far end where the engine would stop—if the train *did* stop, that was. How crossed his fingers and thought hard of the angel, buried in the center of his gas mask. If it really could bring him luck, it had better start doing it now.

The train puffed slowly into the station with a squealing of brakes and a clanking of cars. And it stopped. As it did so, the engine billowed out a cloud of white steam that drifted back along the platform, hiding How in a momentary fog. He hurled himself at the nearest car. Its sides were dauntingly high. He jumped down to the track and scrambled up onto a buffer, covering his hands and knees with grease. Balancing there precariously, he reached up and found he could just get his hands over the car's edge. With a wild scrabble, he found a toehold on the big rivets in the angle iron on the car's corner and clawed his way up.

The car was full of coal. But the level was a few inches down from the top of the car, and How flattened himself on the black lumps, hardly daring to breathe for fear that he had been seen. At any minute, there might be an angry shout from the platform.

None came. The engine gave a piercing whistle and another cloud of steam drifted by above How's hiding place and then, with two or three jerks and a lot of clanking, the train began to move.

Once he judged that they were well clear of the station, How sat up cautiously and rubbed his black hands on the front of his sweater. He seemed to be amazingly high up, and it was very windy. He got a cinder in his eye from the smoke that billowed back over the train. He wiped it with his handkerchief, but it still pricked uncomfortably, causing tears to run down his cheek. The train rattled over a level crossing, and two small children standing there shouted with amusement at the sight of How. Alarmed, he crouched down again. If a sensible adult saw him, the game would be up.

The harsh smell of the coal made How's nose itch, but he dared not sit up again. The train slowed down and stopped at a station, and he lay there quaking with fear again in case the man at Billingborough had rung through to warn the next station that there was a stowaway on board. But the voices that drifted up from the platform sounded no more than conversational, and after a few minutes the guard blew his whistle and the train started off again. How wondered if it stopped many more times before it arrived at Sleaford. He dared not look out at a station to see where he was—and in any case, he knew there was no point in doing that, because the station nameboards had been taken down at the beginning of the war, for fear of helping spies to find their way about.

How felt rather like a spy himself, alone in an unknown country. And suddenly his mind went back to Anna. She had come to an unknown country—she and her German mother. Perhaps people thought *they* were spies. Was that the reason why Auntie Kath was so cross with him for talking to Anna? Was that why Uncle Jack had said, "There's no proof, Kath." Poor Anna, How thought. When he got back, he would make sure nobody was nasty to her again.

He wondered why he was so sure that he *would* come back. At first, he had not liked this strange, flat place. And yet, he had come to enjoy looking out of the window of the small bedroom and seeing the fields with their mist or their frost or their sunshine. At home, his bedroom window looked straight at the window of the house across the street. And besides, there was Anna. And Uncle Jack and Digger, and, in a funny way, there was Billy Thrower. It all added up to a sense of unfinished business.

The train came to a halt again. This time, there was no sound of voices. After a long pause, a locomotive chuffed slowly back past the train on an adjoining line. There were various clunks and bangings, then the train edged forward again, but soon stopped. How lay hidden on top of the coal, wondering if they had come to Sleaford. Somewhere ahead of him, he heard a metallic clang, followed by a slithering rush of something heavy. Risk or no risk, he decided, it was time to investigate.

Very cautiously, he peered over the car's edge and discovered to his horror that the train had been shunted into a coal yard. A gang of men were working their way along it, knocking open the side loading doors of the cars to let the coal pour out. They carried shovels, and a couple of men climbed into each part-emptied car to clear out the last of the coal.

There was no time to be lost. How scrambled over the edge of his car and lowered himself down the outside of its end wall, feeling with his toe for the buffer. Finding it, he crouched there and tossed his gas mask down onto a bit of rough grass on the opposite side from where the men were working. Then he gathered himself and jumped.

His feet slid from under him as he landed on the loose ballast of the track, but he picked himself up, grabbed his gas mask, and ran. He kept running until he was past the end of the train, though he realized with fresh horror that the crew of the shunting engine that now pushed it might have seen him. He saw, too, that he couldn't go across to the station platform as he had vaguely imagined that he would. He was black with coal dust and grease—and he didn't have a ticket, which would have to be explained to the man at the barrier.

He cast a quick glance across the rails and saw that

the station looked like quite a big one. It must be Slea-ford, he thought. The coal yard was bounded by a brick wall, topped by broken glass embedded in cement, but it seemed the only way out, for there were several men standing near a truck at the yard's entrance.

Before he had really thought about it, How was haul-ing his striped sweater over his head. He bundled it tightly and thrust it over the jagged triangles of glass, then scrambled up. He found that there was a road on the other side, with a grass bank under the wall. He jumped down, pulling the sweater after him. It caught on the glass and he tugged at it impatiently, trying to shake it loose. He felt it tear, but he couldn't help that. He tugged again, pulling it down off the wall. His leg hurt, and he saw that blood was trickling from a short gash just above his sock. Carrying his sweater, which had several long, untidy strands of wool dangling from it, he shouldered his gas mask and set off up the road.

Just before the road junction that lay ahead, How came to a stone drinking trough. He washed his hands as best he could in the water that ran from the spout into the trough and held some water to his eye to try and rinse out the cinder, which was still pricking. Then he soaked his handkerchief and mopped at his dirty knees, which were also grazed as a result of his jump from the freight car. Finally, he tied the handkerchief around the cut in his leg and put his sweater on again, chilled by the cold water. Half its sleeve was dangling off. He tucked the loose ends in clumsily and went in search of the main entrance to the station.

Several people looked at How oddly as he walked into the booking hall, but he took no notice. The main worry now was that he might not have enough money for the fare. He joined the line for the ticket office.

"London, please," he said boldly when it came to his turn.

The booking office clerk stared at him suspiciously. "You on your own, son?" he asked.

"Mum always lets me buy my own ticket," said How evasively.

"Single or return?" asked the man, still staring.

"Single," said How. There was no hope of affording a return.

"Seven and tenpence," said the man.

How was ninepence short. "She hasn't given me quite enough," he said and fled. He came to a halt in front of the departures board, scanning it frantically. The next London train left in forty minutes. Forty minutes in which to make ninepence.

With his hands in his pockets and his lips pursed in a casual whistle, How sauntered out of the station, hoping nobody could see how frantic he felt. He glanced around him—and saw, a little way up the street, a sign he recognized from London. It was three brass balls, hanging outside a small shop. He knew the sign meant that the window below it would be crammed with secondhand stuff—coats and clocks and jewelry. And people who sold secondhand things must surely buy them as well. It was his only hope. He walked down the road to the shop and pushed open its door.

112

Inside, the shop was small and dark, crammed with junk of all descriptions. A moose head with huge antlers stared from the wall behind the counter and evening dresses hung from racks. The place smelled strongly of old clothes and slightly mildewed leather.

A very old man in carpet slippers and a cardigan got to his feet and said, "What can I do for you, sonny?"

How had put his gas mask case down on the counter and was hauling out the beaded silk bag and its contents. "There's this ring," he said. "I wanted to sell it."

The old man took the ring from How and screwed a jeweler's glass into his eye, making him look, How thought, as if he was a camera. He inspected the ring closely, then removed the glass and said, "Well, well, well. And how much did you want for this?"

How had been thinking hard. The ring was really quite a pretty one, with its red stone surrounded by little white ones. He would have given it to Anna if it hadn't been much too big for her small fingers. And he needed enough money for the bus fare across London, as well as the ninepence for the train. Dealers always tried to beat you down. He had to try and get at least one and threepence. He frowned with determination and said, "Half a crown."

The old man laughed, and How's heart sank. His journey was going to be stopped before it ever started— and all for a few measly pence. "I've got a few Dinky toys as well," he said, without much hope.

"Don't tempt me," said the old man, chuckling again. Then he stopped laughing and said, "Now, seriously, son, where'd you get this? Are you hocking it for your old man, or your mum? Or did you steal it?"

"No, I *didn't*!" said How, offended. The old man continued to look him in the eye. "Actually," How admitted, "I bought it in an auction, with this bag. Sundry trinkets."

The old man's gaze did not shift. "What did you pay for it?" he asked.

How sighed. The game was up. "Ninepence," he said. "For the lot."

"And what d'you need the money for?" the old man asked.

How hesitated, then gave up. It was no use pretending. And, sooner or later, you had to trust someone. "I've got to get to London," he said. "My mum said she'd write, and she hasn't and I've got to find out what's happened. Dad's in the Army, so he can't. Only I'm ninepence short for the train fare. And then there's the bus."

The old man stared at him thoughtfully, pulling at his lip as if trying to make up his mind about something. Then he said, "All right. Now look, boy, this ring's worth money. Not pennies or shillings—pounds. Is this story of yours true?"

"Yes," said How earnestly. "I've just come from Billingborough in a coal car."

The old man smiled and said, "You look like it!" Then he said, "I tell you what I'll do. I won't *buy* the ring from you, because I don't want you running about on your own in London with a lot of money on you. Someone could pinch it or you might lose it. But I'll lend you some money against it. Would two quid be enough to go on with?"

"Two *pounds*?" How gasped. "Oh, *yes!*"

"Right," said the old man. "What's your name?"

How told him, and the old man wrote him out a ticket and handed it to him with two pound notes. "When you've sorted your business out," he said, "come back to me. Bring your mum or somebody. This ring's only pawned, you understand that?"

"Not really," How admitted.

"You're lending me the ring and I'm lending you two pounds," explained the old man. "It's worth a lot more than that. When you come back, you can pay me back the two pounds—plus a little bit for my trouble—and you can have the ring back. Then you can sell it for the proper price or do whatever you want with it. Now, don't lose that ticket," he went on. "And mind you come back with a grown-up. I'm going to *worry* about you, boy. I'll want to know if this crazy trip of yours turns out all right. So you come back, you hear me? Soon as you can."

"I will," How promised. He folded the pawn ticket and the two pound notes carefully into his pocket and started to repack the bag into his gas mask.

"I reckon you'd better come in here and wash your face before you catch the train," said the old man. "You look like a chimney sweep who's been out in the rain."

"Thanks," said How. This was a real stroke of luck. The angel had done well. For a moment, he thought of showing the little figure to the old man, but decided against it. There was no point in unpacking everything all over again. He had heaps of money now, and if the old man liked the little figure, he might want to buy it. And nothing could make How sell the angel.

NINE

❖

Mr. Bloom, as the old man was called, came back
to the station with How, who felt much better
after a cheese sandwich provided by Mrs. Bloom. She
had also supervised a thorough wash, stuck a bandage
on the cut in his leg and, with a deftly applied hanky,
removed the cinder from his eye. She had brushed the
mud off his shoes and clucked over the tattered state of
his sweater, offering various secondhand coats for How
to try on. "That's the one," she said, as How stood
rather nervously in a double-breasted reefer coat with
an astrakhan collar. "He looks a real little gent."

"Wear it until you come back for the ring," said Mr.
Bloom. And then he had hustled How back to the station, where the man in the booking office gave him a
return ticket to London without comment. He obviously did not recognize the clean and smartly dressed
boy for the ragamuffin who had not had the money for
his fare.

Mr. Bloom found the right platform and pointed out
a compartment with an empty corner seat. How got in,

then lowered the window by its leather strap to lean out and say good-bye.

"Thank you ever so much," he said. He almost blushed now to think that he had expected the old man to beat him down over the price of the ring.

Mr. Bloom shook his head ruefully. "I must be crazy," he said, "turning away a profit like that. Getting old." Then he smiled at How and added, "But I always did like an honest dealer."

The guard blew his whistle.

"Good luck on your journey," said Mr. Bloom. "I'll see you soon."

"Yes, you will," How promised.

The train began to move. Mr. Bloom raised his hand in farewell, then walked away down the platform. How pulled the window up and sat down in his corner seat. After the coal car, it was wonderfully comfortable. The other passengers in the compartment read their newspapers and took no notice of How, but at Grantham, where How changed trains, the London express was much more crowded and he found himself crammed in with a family of young children and their mother. They were on their way to visit their granny in Hampshire, having come down from Scotland, and they were very impressed to hear that How was traveling on his own.

The woman, Mrs. Lennox, obviously assumed that How had come from Grantham, and How kept very quiet about the first stage of his journey. By now, he knew people would be looking for him. Auntie Kath would have discovered his absence, and Digger might have told someone about taking How to the station, though there was a good chance that he might have forgotten it. The porter who had been painting a white line at Billingborough would certainly remember him. How smiled, brushing an imaginary thread from his beautiful coat. Nobody would be looking for a clean, well-dressed boy. But he must be careful. In London, the station staff might well have been told to look out for any child traveling on his own.

Outside, the daylight was fading. The guard came around, pulling down the blinds at all the windows, cutting off the little that could be seen of the flat landscape through the small square left in the middle of the shatterproof protective net pasted on the glass. Mrs. Lennox handed out apples and biscuits to the children, and included How. He joined in a game of *I Spy* for a while, then the youngest toddler fell asleep with his thumb in his mouth, and the game lapsed into silence. How, too, closed his eyes and pretended to be asleep, though his mind was sharply aware of the plushy seat prickling the undersides of his legs, and he was impatient of the train's slow progress and the many stations it stopped at.

When they arrived at last at King's Cross station and Mrs. Lennox opened the door, the familiar smell of London was there, a mixture of smoke and the warm reek of many, many people. How had never noticed it before, but he knew it now as the smell he had grown up in. The youngest child was still asleep, and Mrs. Lennox had to carry him.

"I'll take your case if you like," How offered.

Mrs. Lennox looked relieved. "That would be a help," she said.

How handed her his ticket, having already torn off his return half and tucked it carefully into his shorts pocket.

"If you could hand it in with yours," he said, "I'll have both hands free."

"Yes, of course," said Mrs. Lennox. She distributed various small bags for the children to carry, then they set off in a little group along the dimly lit platform to the barrier. There, How saw, two policemen were standing beside the ticket collector, scrutinizing the people who had come off the train. He tried hard not to look at them.

Mrs. Lennox handed in her handful of tickets, and the ticket collector counted them carefully. "All yours, madam?" he asked, and How's heart was in his mouth in case she told them he was a stranger. But she just said, "We're all together, yes," and they walked through. How felt the nearest policeman glance at him—but then the man resumed his inspection of the passing crowd, looking, How knew, for a boy with muddy shoes and an oversized striped sweater.

He walked with the family through the high-arched hall of the station. The suitcase was heavy and he shifted it from one hand to the other, but he did not mind. His luck had held. The angel was working well.

At the taxi stand, Mrs. Lennox stopped and thanked How for his help. "Is someone meeting you?" she asked.

"No," said How. "I'm just going home."

She looked worried and said, "Where's that?"

"Catford," said How. "I'll get a Number One bus." Secretly, he was wondering where the Number One went to once it came over the bridge. He had never been in this part of London before.

Mrs. Lennox looked more worried than ever and said, "Will you be all right?"

"Oh, yes," said How airily. "The Number One goes up through Waterloo. Or I could get a streetcar from the Embankment."

"We're taking a taxi to Waterloo," said Mrs. Lennox, "to get the train from there on to Granny's. Would you like to come with us?"

How had a moment's wild vision of being an evacuee all over again, with Granny in Hampshire, then realized she just meant Waterloo station. "Oh, yes, please!" he said gratefully. It was almost too good to be true.

The line for taxis was a long one, and How shivered a little in the chilly evening. Mrs. Lennox looked at him and shook her head. "I can't think why nobody's meeting you," she said. "It doesn't seem right."

"I can look after myself," How told her. He hoped she was not going to spoil everything by asking a lot of questions. Another taxi came and went in the darkness, its headlights obscured by the louvered covers that all traffic wore.

"We're next," said How. He had never been in a taxi before, and he was looking forward to it.

A taxi pulled in—and a couple of American soldiers

from farther back in the line made a dive for it. "Piccadilly, bud," one of them said to the driver.

"That's ours!" shouted How.

"Get lost, kid," said the soldier.

How put his head down and barged. He managed to grab the handle of the taxi's door, then shouted to the nearest little girl of the family that surrounded him, "Get in, quick!" The children surged past into the taxi and the driver leaned across to the soldiers and said, "You wait your turn, boys, same as everyone else."

Mrs. Lennox laughed a little breathlessly as they started off and said, "You certainly *can* look after yourself!"

"Well," said How. "Got to, haven't you?" He stared out of the small oblong of clear glass in the middle of the taxi's netted window and tried not to look excited. He liked the nice smell of leather and the tip-up seats on which he and a fat little girl called Josie were sitting. He wondered if the siren had sounded yet. "What's the time?" he asked.

Mrs. Lennox consulted her watch. "Twenty past seven," she said.

How nodded. The raiders didn't come *every* night, he told himself. Perhaps he would go on being lucky. He looked out of the window again, though it was difficult to see anything in the blackout.

"That's Trafalgar Square!" he said as he caught a glimpse of tall sandbagged columns that he recognized as the National Gallery. "You can feed the pigeons there in the daytime."

Josie gazed at him round-eyed and said, "My auntie's got a budgie called Dandy McAllister."

"Our neighbor's got a dog called Bang," How told her with a smile. He felt a lurch of excitement. He would soon be home, and the worry would be over. Here in London, it all felt much better. Probably his mother would be in the middle of writing a letter to him, explaining why she hadn't written before. She would be full of apologies. She had been working full time at the munitions factory, there hadn't been much time. . . . Now that he was so nearly there, How felt almost embarrassed at having come so far and so rashly. He hoped his mother wouldn't be cross.

He saw the river shining darkly below them as they crossed Waterloo Bridge, and a few minutes later they were pulling into the station. They all got out of the taxi and Mrs. Lennox paid the driver. How wondered if he ought to offer to carry the suitcase to her train, but a man in Air Force uniform looked at them and said, "Can I give you a hand?"

"Oh, *thank* you," said Mrs. Lennox. She turned to How and added, "Are you sure you'll be all right, dear?"

"I'll be fine," said How confidently, and he walked away with a jaunty wave, hitching his gas mask onto his shoulder. He dared not admit, even to himself, how small and lonely he felt. Crowds of people packed the station and he did not know where to find the bus stop. He made his way back to the main entrance and walked out the way the taxi had come. Feeling that people would notice him if he stood still and stared around him, he walked briskly down the road, but with mounting panic. He was terribly afraid of getting lost.

A gale of beer fumes came from the doorway of a pub, and a woman stood outside it, smoking a cigarette.

"Excuse me," How said to her politely, "but is this the Waterloo Road?"

The woman flicked ash and said, "Where you trying to go, dear?"

"Catford," said How. "The Number One bus would be best. It goes quite near my house."

"Down there and round the corner," said the woman, pointing. "Cross over the road at the traffic lights and turn right when you get to the other side. Then you go on past the Sally Army hostel, and the stop's along there. What you doing out on your own this time of night?"

"Nothing," said How. "Just going home."

Some sailors came out of the pub singing something very noisily, most of them with bottles in their hands, and How moved away quickly. He found the traffic lights and waited until the small crosscut in the cowling over the lights showed green in the bottom one. He ran across the road in front of the stationary traffic and turned right as he had been told. He passed a doorway with Salvation Army Hostel written above it, and the next bus stop was the one he wanted.

After about ten minutes the bus came and How climbed in, flopping down on the long seat by the parcels space so that he could see out of the doorway and watch for his stop. After all this traveling, it would be awful to go past it in the darkness. With a feeling of triumph, he fished a handful of change out of his pocket and counted out threepence for the bus conductress when she came along. He had done it. He had come home.

He hopped off the bus as it slowed to a halt outside Woolworth's and walked along the street to where his road turned left off it. The bus passed him and went away down the main road, and How broke into a run, putting his hand on his gas mask box to stop it bumping up and down. He turned the corner—and stopped.

It was the smell that warned him first, sharp and dusty. He stared ahead of him, but could make out no details in the darkness. He walked on, and his nostrils prickled with the ominous reck of plaster and earth and splintered wood. Then he saw the gap in the dark line of roofs against the smoky sky. He slowed almost to a halt again, not wanting to know. Perhaps it wasn't his house. "Please," he whispered aloud. "Please."

He looked at the numbers on the terraced houses as he passed them. Nineteen was the Atkinses, twenty-one the Suttons, twenty-three the Ogdens, but their house had wide cracks in its wall, and the door and windows were boarded up.

And then there was nothing.

How stood and stared at the pile of rubble. He could see right through to the mound of earth in the back garden that covered the shelter. The clouds parted in the dark sky and the moon sailed free. Its pale radiance showed the wall of How's bedroom, up there staring at nothing, with its gas fire in the middle of it, and the mantelpiece, and the strangely untorn wallpaper.

The devastation seemed vast, and How realized that the Bells' house that had been on their other side had completely gone as well. He felt himself start to shake. Only a little while ago, he had boasted proudly that he could look after himself. But it wasn't true. The shakiness was so bad that he felt sick. Something gleamed dully in the rubble at his feet. How looked down at it and saw that it was one of the oddly shaped bars from the top of the gas stove. May as well leave it clean, she had said.

Standing there in the street, How began to cry helplessly. And at that moment, the siren sounded.

TEN

◆

How didn't care. Nothing mattered. The raiders had done their worst. The swooping wail of the siren died down to a low-pitched grumble, then faded into silence, and he did not move. It felt as if he would stand there forever.

Something bumped against his legs. It was a dog, he realized. He staggered back slightly as it stood on its hind legs and put its paws against his chest, panting excitedly. It was white, with a pink nose and fawn patches on its ears.

"*Down*, Bang!" someone shouted, then, at closer range, "Oh, my goodness me, that's not Howard, is it?" Doris Ogden was staring at him in concern, with Bang's leash dangling from her hand. "Whatever are you doing here?" she asked.

How shook his head blindly. "I hadn't heard from Mum," he blurted.

"Oh, there," said Doris kindly. "She's all right. She's in the hospital but they say she'll be out in another week." Then she looked at him and added, "Hadn't anyone told you?"

How shook his head again, but this time, in the midst of his tears, he felt a wild relief. She was all right.

In the distance, there was a low grumble of gunfire. The long beam of a searchlight swung across the sky and was joined by a second one, lighting up the underside of the clouds.

"You can't stay out here," said Doris. "Come on." With How at her side, she started down the street. He wondered vaguely where they were going, but it didn't seem to matter much. He still felt shaky. "Where have you come from?" asked Doris.

"Lincolnshire," said How. "From Auntie Kath's. On the train."

"What, all by yourself?" Doris looked startled. "But where are you going to stay tonight?"

"I don't know," said How. Mrs. Armstrong's house was in a terrible mess as well, he noticed, with no doors or windows or roof.

Doris paused and whistled for the dog, which had stopped to sniff at a lamppost. "You'd better have your leash on," she said, and bent down to clip the leash to Bang's collar. "It wasn't fleas," she added to How as they started off again. "We got the Council man in, and he said it was bedbugs. Nothing to do with dogs. He said they're getting to be an awful nuisance in shelters now. He treated it all around with paraffin."

The gunfire was getting louder, and How could hear the distant, vibrating drone of a lot of aircraft engines.

"They say they'll repair our house," Doris went on a little breathlessly as they hurried on. "Only they're so busy, we'll have to wait a bit. So we're living in the public shelter for now. It's awful, really. You never feel clean. They bring those mobile showers around, but it's not the same. But at least there's toilets."

How nodded. He had seen the tanker trucks with a tent behind them standing in the street, with a line of people waiting, each one with a towel and an armful of clean clothes, and he always felt sorry for the bombed-out people who had to use them. He had never thought he might be one of them.

A tin-hatted Air Raid Warden passed them and said, "Get under cover, quickly."

Doris and How broke into a run, with the dog galloping beside them. They dived into the sandbagged entrance to the public shelter just as the nearest batteries of antiaircraft guns opened up with a series of deafening explosions. They pushed through the black curtains into the crowded interior, where people sat on benches on either side of the narrow entrance. Small light bulbs at intervals in the low concrete ceiling gave a dim light, and the smell of crowded people was warm and thick. A baby was crying loudly and somewhere from deeper in the shelter came a dragged-out chorus of "Roll Out the Barrel." Large black letters stenciled on the wall acted as a system of street names in the underground network of shelters.

"We're in B3," said Doris, picking her way through the crowds. Children were being settled for the night under rugs and blankets on the benches.

There was a serious outbreak of fuss from Mr. and

Mrs. Ogden when Doris arrived with How. They seemed to think that something should be done about him, and after much talk about "letting the authorities know," Mrs. Ogden went off and came back with a stout lady in the dark green uniform of the WVS, who looked at How very much as Auntie Kath would have done and said, "Well, young man. A nice lot of bother you've caused us all."

"I'm sorry," said How meekly. "I'll go back to Auntie Kath's tomorrow. I've got my return ticket. Only I'd like to see Mum first."

"I'll take him," said Doris. "We can go to afternoon visiting time. Poor lamb, he can't go back without seeing her."

"Why wasn't she in a shelter?" asked the WVS lady rather severely.

"She was on late shift at the factory," Mrs. Ogden explained, "and she stopped there for a meal in the canteen. By the time she got the bus back here, the siren had gone off. Well, I mean, none of us take much notice of that, do we? So she went into the house, I suppose to have a wash and that, before she went over to Mrs. Armstrong's shelter, and then the guns started up. She ran across the road, but she was too late. Got caught in the street. Janice Hogg told me all about it. She works at the hospital." She pursed her lips and added, "If Muriel had been down in the shelter with us, it would never have happened."

"No use iffing," said the WVS lady briskly. "There's obviously been a mix-up somewhere, otherwise this young man would have been told what had happened. I'll notify the police that he's been found—there'll be a lot of people worrying about him. Now, what are we going to do? Can you take charge of him for tonight, or shall I make other arrangements?"

Mr. Ogden said firmly, "He'd better stay here. We can all shove up a bit, make enough room."

"Good," said the lady. "I'll give you an emergency blanket. Oh, and I'll want the address of this aunt in Lincolnshire." And she bustled off.

How yawned suddenly, and Doris looked at him and said, "Poor kid, he must be worn out. Listen, How, if you want to use them, the toilets are down the end of C4. Pop along there, and we'll sort out a bed for you."

"Thanks," said How. He found that he ached all over with tiredness. He picked his way through the crowded shelter, stepping over people who had lain down to sleep on the ground. An old lady was putting a cloth over a birdcage with a parrot in it. "Night-night, Polly," she was saying. "Sleep tight."

When he got back to B3, How wrapped himself in the red blanket provided by the WVS lady and lay down on a rug, with Mr. Ogden's rolled-up jacket as a pillow. Bang was curled up beside him in his basket. The ground was very hard, and the singers in A2 were bawling out a lusty version of "Lili Marlene," but he didn't care. In a few minutes, he was fast asleep.

In the morning, How woke up feeling stiff and cramped. He turned on his other side and tried to go to sleep again, but it was no good. He sat up and yawned, rubbing his eyes.

"Hello," said a familiar voice. "I heard you were back."

Clifford stood in front of him, earnest and bespectacled as always. How grinned and said, "News gets around. Is this the shelter you sleep in, then?"

"Yes, we've always come here," said Clifford. "But you knew that, didn't you?"

How thumped himself on the forehead. "Of course!" he said. "I just didn't realize it was this shelter we were coming to. Everything was in such a muddle last night."

Doris sat up and yawned. "Hello, dear," she said. "You found a little friend."

Clifford wrinkled his nose at this description and said, "My name's Clifford Lee, actually. And my mother said How can come and spend the day with us if he likes. We live in the flat over the pharmacist's."

"Crowhurst's?" asked Doris.

Clifford nodded and said, "That's right."

"Sounds like a good idea," said Doris. She glanced at her sleeping parents and added, "I shouldn't think Mum will mind. What about going to the hospital, How? Shall I pick you up after lunch? Say about two?"

"That would be lovely," said How gratefully.

He and Clifford made their way through the fusty-smelling shelter to its entrance. Outside, the bare plane trees reached their arms into a pale sky. It seemed a long way off, up above the buildings. You could see no

132

horizons in London. It was odd, How thought, that he had never noticed that before.

"Did you run away by train?" asked Clifford.

"Yes," said How, and told him all about it. "And I brought some Dinky toys for you, too," he ended. "They're in my gas mask case."

"Thanks," said Clifford. "I owe you sixpence, but I haven't actually got it." After a pause, he added, "I suppose you didn't happen to notice what locomotive it was on your train to London?"

How laughed. "I knew you'd ask that," he said. "I don't know about the one that pulled the coal cars, but from Grantham it was an engine called Coldstreamer. Number 4844." He felt rather pleased with himself for having noticed this, but Clifford looked faintly disappointed and said, "Seen it. They're nice, though, those Green Arrows."

They walked on down the street. "What's it like in the country?" asked Clifford curiously. "Is it awful? Is that why you ran away?"

"No, I had to come home because I was worried about Mum," How explained. "She promised she'd write, and she didn't."

"She might have," Clifford pointed out. "Letters don't always get through. Dad said the main sorting office got hit last week. He saw it when he was driving his ambulance. Heck of a fire, he said."

"I never thought of that," said How. Increasingly, he felt rather guilty about causing so much trouble.

"Are you going to stay here?" asked Clifford. "I mean, have you come back for good?"

How shook his head. "I can't," he said. He had no home in London now. But in any case, he had to go back, to see old Mr. Bloom about the unbelievable business of the ring, and then to see Anna, and make his apologies to Auntie Kath and Uncle Jack.

Clifford looked at him seriously and said, "I could ask Mum if you could stay with us. Just until your mother's out of hospital."

"Thanks," said How. "But I couldn't do that."

"You like it, don't you," said Clifford with a trace of accusation. "The country, I mean. You've taken to it."

A pigeon strutted across the pavement and pecked at a brown, withered apple core, and How thought suddenly of the water that ran sparkling in the dike outside Auntie Kath's house. With an odd sense of surprise, he found that Clifford was right. He had taken to it. He shrugged and did not know what to say.

Doris came to collect How after lunch, and they set off from Clifford's apartment on foot, with Bang on the leash. "It's not very far to the hospital," Doris said, "and we can go across the park. Makes a nice change from that blooming old shelter."

"Have they said when you can move back into the house?" asked How.

"It'll be about a month, they think," said Doris. "It's got to be shored up with timber. I'm really sick of this war," she added. "I'd treated myself to a really nice hat just the day before our bomb dropped, and I never even got a chance to wear it."

"Shame," said How.

They stopped at the hospital gate to buy a bunch of daffodils for How's mother and to tie Bang's leash to the railings. "*Stay*," said Doris sternly. "Good boy. I won't be long."

The echoing corridors and the smell of disinfectant made How feel nervous. He had been trying not to wonder whether his mother was very badly injured, but now he was about to find out.

The double doors that led to the ward had circular windows in them, too high up for How to see through them. They swung to behind him and Doris, and he found himself in a big, high-windowed room with long rows of beds on either side. There were several tables down the middle of the room with flowers on them, and there was a lidded tank that sent up a wisp of steam.

"That's a sterilizer," said Doris knowledgeably. "Now, where is she?"

A nurse in a dark blue uniform bustled toward them. "I'm Sister Pugh," she said. "Mrs. Grainger, is it? She's in the next bed to the end, down there on the right." Then she looked at How and added, "We don't really allow children."

How clenched his fists by his sides and said, "You've *got* to."

Sister Pugh looked at him. "Well," she said, "just this once, if it's urgent. No sitting on the beds, mind."

How nodded absently. He was staring down the line

of beds, trying to see his mother. All the patients wore white hospital nightdresses with buttons down the front, and most of them looked very old. There were visitors sitting by almost every bed. He started down the ward, with Doris following.

The last bed but one had a soldier sitting beside it, his back turned to How as he talked to the woman in the bed, holding her hand. Her head was swathed in a white turban of bandages, covering one eye, so that for a moment How was not sure who she was. Then he knew, and ran toward her.

His mother gave a cry of surprise and held out her arms and, ignoring Sister Pugh's instructions, How sat on the bed and hugged her. "Are you all right?" he asked.

"Yes, love, I'm fine," said his mother. "Fancy you turning up like this! Where's Auntie Kath? Did she bring you? Oh, hello, Doris, you, too? Oh, and daffies, how lovely! My goodness, aren't I having a day! Say hello to your dad, How—I don't believe you've seen who it is, have you?"

How turned and looked at the soldier who sat by the bed, and it was his father who smiled back at him, with his forage cap tucked under the shoulder strap of his khaki battledress tunic.

"Dad!" he gasped.

"All right, are you?" said his father, and How laughed at this echo of the phrase Uncle Jack always used. "Oh, *yes!*" he said.

"I'm on compassionate leave," said his father. "They

let me have four days when the news came through about your mum being hurt."

"You shouldn't have come all that way, How," scolded his mother, smiling all the same. "Such an expense for Auntie Kath. I said in my letter I'd be out in a week or so and not to worry."

How shook his head. "I never got a letter," he said. "And Auntie Kath didn't bring me."

His mother and father looked at each other in consternation, and Doris said, "I was out with the dog last night and found him standing by the house—or what's left of it. Crying his heart out, poor lamb. He'd come all the way from Lincolnshire on his own. Do you believe it?"

"You don't have to worry," How said quickly. "A policeman came to Clifford's this morning, where I was, and I told him all about it. And I told the WVS lady last night, and she said they'd let Auntie Kath know."

His father shook his head. "What a thing to do," he said. "What a boy."

How's mother was quiet for a moment, staring at him. Then she said, "It's all too much. And where did you get that coat? Is it one of Uncle Jack's auction sale buys?"

"No," said How. There was such a lot of explaining to do. He fished in the coat's big pocket and hauled out the silk blouse, which he had carefully folded small so that it would fit. "This is for you," he said. "I'm sorry if it's a bit crumpled."

"Oh, it's lovely!" said his mother, holding it up.

"Looks like pure silk," said Doris.

There was a moment's pause, then they all started to say something, and all stopped. How's mother laughed and leaned her head back against her pillows. "So much to talk about," she said.

Doris got up and said, "I'm going to take Bang for a run. I don't like leaving him tied up."

"Mum, it wasn't fleas," said How. "It was—" He had forgotten what they were called.

"Bedbugs," said Doris.

How's mother reached up and took her hand. "Doris, love, I'm ever so sorry," she said. "Whatever they were, I oughtn't to have got on my high horse about it. It's just this—"

"This blooming old war," said Doris. "I know. It's all right, honest. See you a bit later." And she gave them a cheery wave and walked off down the ward.

"Such a nice girl, really," said How's mother. She sounded tired. How stared at her. The turban of bandages worried him. Why did it cover her eye? Hesitantly, he asked, "What sort of hurt is it?"

"Oh, it's just a cut on the head," said his mother lightly. "Silly thing really. But it was just across my eye, and they thought I wouldn't be able to see out of it, so they did an operation to tidy it up. It's much better now. They say it'll leave a bit of a scar, but that doesn't matter, does it? I was never much of a glamour girl, anyway."

How smiled and shook his head and felt terribly close

to tears again. His father put his arm around How's shoulders and looked at his wife. "We're lucky you're alive, love," he said.

"We've had lots of luck," said How. He was digging in his pocket again, this time for the most important thing of all, transferred from his gas mask case this morning when he had given Clifford the Dinky toys. "This is the angel," he said, and put the little figure into his father's hand. "He brought the luck." But, at the back of his mind, he heard Stanley saying, "That Anna Rose, she's bad luck, she is." And Uncle Jack had fallen off the ladder, and Auntie Kath had lost her purse, and there had been all sorts of small unlucky things at school. Perhaps the angel had given How so much luck that he had taken more than his share, and other people had to be unlucky to balance it.

His father was examining the little figure carefully. "Where on earth did you get this?" he asked. "It's very old—Roman, I should think." He held it out to How, returning it, but How hesitated, then shook his head.

"You keep it," he said. "It's your turn now. If you're going back to the war—you need the luck."

His father looked at him gravely. "Thanks," he said. "I'll take great care of it." He unbuttoned the breast pocket of his tunic and got out a khaki handkerchief, wrapped the little figure carefully in it and buttoned it back into his pocket. "There," he said. "Safe."

How smiled at him. In an odd sort of way, he felt relieved.

"What are we going to do?" asked his mother fretfully. "How can't stay in London with no home to go to—and what's going to happen when I get out of here? Where are we going to live? I suppose it'll have to be one of those hostels, or else the public shelter."

How's father put his hand over hers. "Don't you worry, love," he said. "I don't have to go back until Wednesday, and it's only Sunday today. There's plenty of time to get things sorted out. I'll take How back to Jack and Kath tomorrow, and have a word with them—and Sister says when you leave here you'll be going to a convalescent home for a bit, until you're properly better. So there's no hurry."

How's mother was still trying to make plans. "I could keep going over to Kitty Armstrong's shelter at night," she said.

How's father did not answer. How looked at him and knew that something was wrong, and so did his mother.

"What's the matter?" she asked.

"I don't know if I ought to tell you, love," said How's father. "But you'll have to know sooner or later. There was a whole stick of bombs, you see—a man in the pub told me. One got the garage on the corner, then there was one in the road, and the next one was ours. But the one after that was behind Kitty's house, in the garden."

How's mother put her hand to her mouth. "The shelter," she said.

"Kitty can't have known anything about it," said

How's father. "With a direct hit like that, it's all over in a second. But you see what I mean, love, when I say we're lucky you're alive. If you hadn't been late coming home from work, you'd have been in that shelter, too."

"Kitty," whispered How's mother. Her face was very white under her bandages.

How thought of Mrs. Armstrong, who wore black lace-up shoes and had fat legs, and knew he should feel upset. But he just felt angry. "I wish I was old enough to be a soldier," he said.

His father looked at him and said, "I'm glad you're not, son. I know what you mean—you want the whole thing to be over and done with, and so do I. But after that, we're really going to need you."

"Me?" said How, surprised.

"You and all the other kids who are growing up," said his father. "There's going to be a lot to do. You've learned to think for yourselves in this war. Maybe when you run things, you'll know better than we did—make sure we don't get landed in another lot of trouble."

How nodded gravely. He wasn't exactly sure what his father meant, but he felt very grown-up and important.

"I don't know what Auntie Kath's going to say," said How's mother, who had not really been listening. "It's all such a muddle. Why did you run away like that? I want to know all about it."

"Yes," said How. And he told her.

■ ■ ■

Doris came back when the bell rang for the end of visiting time, and they all kissed How's mother good-bye.

"You be a good boy," she said, hugging How tightly while Sister Pugh looked with disapproval at the rumpled bed. "Give my love to Auntie Kath and Uncle Jack. I'll try and come up there soon, to see you."

"That would be lovely," said How. And then Sister Pugh pushed everyone out, and they were walking down the echoing corridor in the bright light of its overhead bulbs in their metal shades. Outside, it was nearly dark and Bang whined impatiently on his leash by the railings.

"What are we going to do now?" asked How, wondering if his father's arrival had changed everything.

"We're all going back to your friend Clifford's," said Doris firmly. "My mum and dad are coming over there to tea. Then we'll see."

How smiled at her gratefully and felt sorry that, in all those months of nights in the shelter, he had never realized how nice she was. Perhaps it was because her mother snored so loudly.

It was a jolly evening. Clifford's father played the piano and they all sang songs, and then How was packed off upstairs to have a bath. After Auntie Kath's tin bath in front of the fire, with jugs of water heated in the kitchen, it was wonderfully luxurious to have hot water coming out of a tap. He put on a pair of Clifford's pajamas and went downstairs, where Mrs. Lee was making a flask of tea to take down in the shelter. The Ogdens had already gone.

The "regulars" in the shelter all had their permanent places, so there wasn't room for How and his father beside Clifford's family. They slept up in F2, where an old man snored even more loudly than Mrs. Ogden, but How didn't mind. Somehow, he was quite sure now that everything was going to be all right.

ELEVEN

◆

I tell you," said Mr. Bloom as he fitted a key into a small jewelry case, "that's quite a boy you've got there."

"You can say that again," agreed How's father. "Half of the police in England looking for him, and he manages to get all that way."

"My wife thought I should report that I'd seen him," said Mr. Bloom, squinting thoughtfully at the ring, "and I don't mind telling you, I nearly did. But I thought, no, I'll give him a chance. This is a nice ring, you know. Quite a good ruby, set with small diamonds. I'll give you a good price for it if you want to sell it."

How and his father looked at each other, then they both shook their heads. "No," said Mr. Bloom, "I didn't think you would." He looked over his glasses at How and added, "What about that coat, boy? Do you want to keep it?"

How held his arms away from his sides, looking down at the coat, then shook his head. It was nice, but Billy Thrower would laugh at it. And besides, it was too heavy to wear for things like climbing into the secret hayloft.

"Don't be daft," said his father. "You can keep it for best." He picked up the ring and added, "Now, Mr. Bloom, what do we owe you?"

"Say fifteen bob for the coat," said the old man, "and two pounds back on the ring, plus the commission— say two pounds seventeen and six."

How's father put three pound notes on the counter and said, "I don't want any change. I can't thank you enough for what you did for How. He was lucky to find you."

"That boy will always be lucky," said Mr. Bloom.

From Sleaford, they caught the bus back to Billingborough.

"It reminds me of when I was a kid," said How's father, staring out across the fields. "I miss it, in a way. You get used to the sky being so big."

How nodded. "You can't see much of it in London," he said.

They relapsed into silence, then How said a little nervously, "Does Auntie Kath know we're coming?"

"Yes, I sent her a telegram from London," said his father.

"Oh," said How. That must have been expensive, he thought. He undid his coat and dug in his shorts pocket.

"What are you looking for?" asked his father.

"You paid Mr. Bloom for the ring," said How, "and my coat and everything. That's not fair." He put a handful of money in his father's hand, the coins wrapped in the remaining pound note. "There should be one pound nineteen and fourpence halfpenny," he said. Clifford had given him three-halfpence for the Dinky toys.

"If you think I'm taking that, you're off your chump," said his father firmly, returning the money. "You earned it, you keep it." After a pause, he added, "I was glad you didn't want to sell the ring. What do you think we should do with it?"

How looked at him. "Give it to Mum," he said.

His father smiled. "That's what I'd like to do with it, too," he said. "Good old boy. I'll give it to her tomorrow."

"Right," said How.

They got off the bus in Billingborough, and How clutched at his father's arm. "Look!" he said. "There's Digger!"

Digger shambled toward them, beaming. "Mr. Grainger can't come," he said.

"I know," said How. "He can't drive the truck until his shoulder's better."

"My dad come instead," said Digger, waving an arm. "With the pony."

Along the street, How saw the piebald pony harnessed to a dogcart. Digger's father, standing at the pony's head, waved a hand in greeting.

"What a reception!" said How's father. "Marvelous!" He heaved his pack into the back of the cart and held the tailgate open for Digger and How to climb in, then got up beside Mr. Bailey, who clucked to the pony to start it moving.

How slipped the string of his gas mask box off his shoulder and opened it, unfolding the straps and the eyepiece. The familiar whiff of rubber wafted up to him, mixed with the stale scent of violets. There was only one thing left inside. He took out the beaded black silk bag and handed it to Digger. "That's for you," he said.

Digger stared at it speechlessly, then stroked it gently with a black-nailed finger. "That's beautiful," he breathed. "Beautiful, that is." He pressed it to his face. "Smell of flowers," he said.

How nodded, smiling.

"I got a special place for it," Digger told him. "A right special place."

"That's nice," said How. He could see clearly in his mind's eye the way Digger would rearrange the junk on the bench in his father's shed to make room for the bag. He smiled again. In a way, he felt sad about Digger—but, he thought, you couldn't be sorry for him. Digger was so happy.

There were daffodils budding in the cottage gardens. How thought of the daffodils Doris had bought at the hospital gate, long-stemmed and leafless in their vase on the locker beside his mother's bed. Greenhouse, most probably, he thought with a sniff of contempt. Not like these, growing fat and strong in the black soil.

He caught snatches of conversation from the driving

seat in front of him, though the rasp of the cart's wheels and the clip-clop of the pony's feet made it difficult to hear much. The words "raider" and "bullet" were mentioned. Most probably Mr. Bailey was telling tales of his time in the Navy, How thought, like Uncle Jack was apt to talk about the First World War.

Digger's father brought the pony to a halt outside Auntie Kath's house. Uncle Jack was in the garden, weeding cabbages one-handedly, though How saw that his arm was no longer in a sling. He straightened up and came to the gate as How's father jumped down from the dogcart. They grinned at each other, and How saw for the first time that they were very alike, although Uncle Jack was so much older. "Hello, traveler," Uncle Jack said to him. "All right, are you?"

Auntie Kath had made Irish stew with dumplings, and although she looked at How and shook her head, she did not scold him. Stanley was not there, and How realized that he must be at school. It did not feel a bit like a Monday.

There was a syrupy sweet custard for dessert. "As to your foreign friends," Auntie Kath said as she handed How a huge helping, "they've come out in their true colors all right. Nice goings on, I must say."

"Why?" asked How with a stab of alarm. "What's happened?"

"Well may you ask," said Auntie Kath grimly. "More custard?"

"No, thank you," said How. "But what *happened*?"

Auntie Kath pursed her lips. "Signaling to the en-

148

emy," she said. "No wonder we got shot up."

"Shot up?" How was beginning to feel like a parrot. "What do you mean?"

His father looked at him and said, "You wouldn't have heard. Mr. Bailey was telling me. Apparently a daylight raider got through. Heaven knows what it was looking for, it must have been miles off course. But it opened up with a machine gun, right along the village street. Nobody was hurt, though."

"The kiddies were at Sunday School," said Auntie Kath virtuously. "Yesterday morning, it was. A bullet went in between two girls and stuck in the floor. The policeman tried to get it out, but it'd jammed in that tight, he couldn't."

"Oh, no, he won't shift that," said How's father. "Silly to try. What's all this about signaling to the enemy, though? I don't think Ben Bailey had heard about that."

"There were lights burning in that old house Howard's so fond of," said Auntie Kath. "Bold as brass. And all sorts of funny goings on. A ram's skull, they found, and a dagger. We know who's responsible for *that*, don't we?"

"I still say there's no proof," said Uncle Jack obstinately.

Auntie Kath turned on him. "How much more proof do you want?" she demanded. "Their cottage is only just across the fields from the old house—poky little place it is, too, stuck out in the middle of nowhere."

"But what happened?" asked How again.

"Percy Barker was coming home on his bike down the back lane after a darts match," said Auntie Kath. "And he saw this light, up in the old house. Well, he had a job getting in there, it's so overgrown, but he found a gap in the railings around the back—and there's a path, he said, leading right from that gap to *their* cottage, straight across the fields, so you could see they'd been coming in. And he found seven candles—*seven*, mind you—burning around a ram's skull, with horns like the Devil. And a dagger laid in front of it. Well, he blew the candles out, of course, and came straight back here and told the policeman, Jim Bowker. But the damage had been done. That was the Saturday night, and the very next morning, we get this raider."

"It wasn't Anna," said How as Auntie Kath fixed him with an accusing eye. "I know it wasn't. She wouldn't."

"Then you know something the rest of us don't," said Auntie Kath. "Why would she run away if she hadn't done something she was ashamed of?"

How stared at her. "What do you mean?" he asked stupidly.

Uncle Jack looked unhappy. "They took Mrs. Rose in for questioning," he said. "And Mrs. Bowker—that's the policeman's wife—kept the little girl with her, to keep an eye on her, like, while her mother was at the police station in Billingborough."

"Out of the pantry window and away," said Auntie Kath, tucking in her double chins with disapproval. "Never seen hair nor hide of her since, and that was yesterday dinnertime."

How stared at his dessert, suddenly feeling that he couldn't eat another mouthful. He wanted to get up from the table at once, and run and run until he reached the hayloft. That's where she would be.

His father looked at him as if guessing what was in his mind, though How had not said anything about Anna or their secret place. "I reckon we'll go and have a look around after lunch, shall we?" he said. "I'd like to see this old house, anyway. Sounds interesting."

How nodded dumbly. A terrible dilemma had presented itself. If he wanted to find Anna, was it right to betray the secret of their hiding place?

Later that afternoon, he took his father down the lane and across the fields the way Billy Thrower had shown him, up the path along the field's edge and across the fallen tree into the garden of the old house.

"What a place!" said How's father, surveying it from among the tangle of elder and bramble. "Beautiful. They knew how to build in those days. Who does it belong to, How, do you know?"

"Uncle Jack says the owner died," said How, "and his daughter lives in London somewhere." He led the way to the door that stood ajar. Inside, seven half-burned candles with blackened wicks stood around the ram's skull. How frowned at them. "Those weren't there before," he said. "There was only one—a little stub."

"Funny, isn't it," said his father. He fingered the corroded metal blade that lay on the bricks in front of the skull. How frowned over that as well. There was something half-familiar about it, and yet it was a very alien object. Anna would never have imported a thing of that sort.

"There's certainly *something* going on," said How's father. He turned to the door that led to the hall and the stairway.

"Look out!" How shouted suddenly—but it was too late. The rusty bucket that he had seen balanced on top of the half-open door came crashing down, narrowly missing his father, and clattered noisily across the brick floor. How's father had leapt out of the way. "Lucky that didn't land on my head," he said. "Somebody doesn't want us in this place."

How said nothing.

His father came back and looked at him seriously in the dim light that filtered through the ivy-clad windows. "Look," he said, "I know it's your business, and I don't want to interfere. But this isn't a joke, is it. Whatever's going on, it's pretty serious."

How nodded miserably.

"This little girl's a friend of yours, isn't she?" said his father.

How nodded again.

"Then, honestly, if you know where she might be, I think we ought to try and find her," his father went on. "You see, she could be in some danger, How."

After an agonized pause, How turned and headed wordlessly for the hall. His father was right. He led the way to the side door that opened onto the yard, but his father stopped and glanced up the stairs. "Nasty gap in the banisters up there," he said. "Someone could easily fall through. You won't use this house as a place to play in, How, will you? If you had an accident here, nobody would know."

"I don't want to play that sort of game," said How in truth, and he lugged the side door open. There was no sign of a face at the little window high up in the gable. Anna would have heard the bucket fall, he thought. That's why she put it there, so she would know if anyone came through the house, looking for her. She would have bolted the trap door. He could almost see her, sitting up there in the hayloft with her arms hugging her knees, frightened.

He led the way into the stable and climbed up from the manger to the hayrack. To his surprise, the trap door lifted easily. Had she forgotten to bolt it?

"Anna," he said, "it's all right. It's only me."

Dust motes danced slowly in the shaft of sunlight that came in from the high window. The flowers in the jar on the shawl-covered table were dead. The ring of blue glass beads lay in an empty circle where the angel had been. But it had come back now, How thought desperately. It was only a few feet away, in his father's pocket. "Anna!" he called again, though he knew she was not there.

He let the trap door back into its place and climbed down to the stable floor, where he stood looking crestfallen. "I was sure she'd be there," he said.

"Perhaps she's looking for *you*," suggested his father.

"She can't have gone back home—Jack says they've put a police guard on the cottage."

How shook his head speechlessly.

His father smiled at him and patted his tunic pocket. "Come on, angel," he said. "Do your stuff."

But How could not smile back.

He took his father up to the Holy Well and showed him where Anna had been sitting on that Sunday afternoon that now seemed so long ago. Secretly, he had hoped that she might be there again, but the place was empty and deserted, and the water ran clear and sparkling in the little spring as it had always done, not knowing who came and went, or what happened to them.

How and his father walked slowly home.

Auntie Kath had prepared an early tea—sardines on toast and sticky buns—and while they ate, there was a conversation between the grown-ups that How would have found very exciting if he hadn't been so worried about Anna.

"We always did say we'd go into business together after the war," Uncle Jack was saying. "Grainger Brothers—Builders. And the old place is ideal for it, as you say. Got plenty of space."

"Being L-shaped," said How's father, "it would convert into two houses with no bother at all, one for you and one for us. And we'd put proper modern plumbing in."

"You mean I could have a bathroom?" asked Auntie

Kath. "With running hot and cold, and tiles on the wall?" She clasped her hands excitedly.

"And a decent kitchen, too," said Uncle Jack. "You deserve it, girl. You've been a good wife to me."

"We'll have the compensation money for the bomb damage," said How's father, "and the old house is in pretty bad shape, so it shouldn't be too expensive. With us both chipping in, we should be all right."

"It's only a couple of daft builders who'd take it on," said Uncle Jack with a rare grin. He turned to How and added, "What do you think of that? D'you like the idea of us buying the old house?"

"Your mum would be pleased," put in Auntie Kath before How could answer. "Poor soul, she must be wondering where she's going to find a roof over her head."

"Yes," said How. "It sounds lovely."

But would it be? In his mind's eye, he could see them living in the house, but haunted by the small, dark-eyed ghost of Anna.

His father looked out of the window and said, "There's Ben Bailey with the dogcart."

"Time goes so fast," fretted Auntie Kath. "We've hardly seen you, Fred, and now you've got to go back."

"Better than nothing," said Uncle Jack. He turned to How and added, "Do you want to go into Billingborough with your dad and see him on the bus?"

"Yes, please," said How.

At that moment, he saw Stanley nudge the garden gate open with his bicycle's front wheel and ride up the path. He waved, and Stanley dumped his bike against the willow tree and came in through the back door.

"Hello, Uncle Fred!" Stanley said to How's father, then rushed on with his news. "Here, they let that woman go! Couldn't prove it, they said. Would you believe that?"

"No!" said Auntie Kath. "Are you sure?"

"Certain," said Stanley. "Jim Bowker's little kid's in the infants, and she goes home for lunch, and she told everyone when she came back this afternoon."

"*Mr.* Bowker to you, young man," said Auntie Kath reprovingly, but she was too interested to be cross. "Fancy that!" she said.

How's father glanced at the clock on the mantelpiece and said, "I'll have to go, I'm afraid, if I'm going to get that bus from Billingborough. Otherwise I'll miss the train at Sleaford and I won't get back tonight."

Everyone went out to the dogcart. How was a little disappointed to see that Digger wasn't there. He was always friendly, even if he didn't always understand what was going on.

"Digger? He's been mucking out pigsties this afternoon," said Mr. Bailey. "You wouldn't want him sitting beside you, not smelling like that. I left him in a bath in front of the fire."

How had a ridiculous vision of Digger playing with a rubber duck in his bath and smiled for the first time since lunch.

Waiting for the bus, his father put an arm around How's

156

shoulders and gave him a hug. "I'm sorry I've got to go," he said. "But you can see the way things are."

"Yes," said How. "Don't forget to give Mum the ring."

"You bet," said his father. After a pause, he added, "Try not to worry about your friend too much. I expect she'll make her way home now they've let her mother go."

"Yes," said How.

"There's a lot of silly things happen in a war," his father told him. "You mustn't let them get you down."

"No," said How.

The bus was coming along the street, and his father stooped for his pack. "There's a lot to look forward to," he said.

How nodded.

"It won't be as long as you think," said his father. He waved at Mr. Bailey and gave How a wink, then got on the bus.

"See you soon," he said.

"Yes," said How. He waved until the bus had disappeared around the corner. Then he walked back to Mr. Bailey, who was sitting patiently on the driving seat of the dogcart, with a rug over his knees against the chilly air of the late afternoon.

TWELVE

❖

As they clip-clopped back along the lanes in the ebbing daylight, How was thinking hard. Where could Anna have got to? She might not know that her mother had been released. Night was coming on, and she would need shelter. He stared across the fields, almost imagining that he could see her small figure walking along by the dike against the darkening sky. Once, he turned his head sharply, thinking he had seen something move, but it was only a black dog running along the bank under the leafless hedge.

Anna would not come back, How thought, until she knew it had been proved that she and her mother had nothing to do with the light in the old house. But Anna could not ask for news. As a runaway, she would not dare to approach anyone. Even at the best of times, she was afraid of people. "Animals don't do you any harm," she had said, meaning that people could, and often did. How desperately wanted to know whether she had found her way home.

The dogcart turned into the lane that led to Auntie Kath's house, and a half-realized idea was in his mind, complete. He said impetuously, "I can walk from here, Mr. Bailey."

"Reckon you can," said the old man readily. "Tell you the truth, I'll be glad to get back home. This cold wind plays my knees up something chronic."

How jumped down from the dogcart and watched Mr. Bailey back the pony to the junction of the lanes and set off in the opposite direction. Then he took to his heels and ran until he came to the turning across the fields, where he slowed a little because of the heavy clods of earth, which made the going more difficult. When he came to the fallen tree, he did not cross it but veered left, to keep to the field's edge. It would be quicker this way, he thought, than going through the old house. Anna's cottage lay on this side of the tangled garden, almost in a straight line from where he was walking now. He had seen it from the hayloft window, half hidden among trees.

He came to the narrow path that led off across the fields, panting a little, and started to run again. He must not be too late back, or Auntie Kath would ask questions.

At last he came to the cottage gate and pushed it open. The garden inside was not unkempt as he had somehow expected. The big clumps of plants had been clipped back tidily and a black cat with white paws sat on the doorstep and watched How approach. It stood up and rubbed against his legs as he rapped on the door with his knuckles.

He heard quick footsteps inside. The door was

opened and the cat ran in past a small woman whose dark hair was coiled into a bun on the nape of her neck. She clutched a handkerchief in her hand and stared at How from eyes as dark as Anna's. In the last of the daylight, How thought she looked as if she had been crying.

"My name's Howard Grainger," he said. "I'm a friend of Anna's. I just wondered—"

There was no need to finish the question. Mrs. Rose shook her head, and tears filled her eyes again. "When I was hearing you knock," she said in her strange English, "I was thinking perhaps it was her."

"I'm sorry," said How wretchedly. "I just couldn't go home without knowing."

Mrs. Rose gave a tremulous smile. "You are a kind boy," she said. "Please, will you come in? Perhaps you will like some coffee?"

How shook his head. "Thank you very much, but I've got to go home," he said. "I mean, to my Auntie Kath's. It's nearly dark and she'll be worrying."

"Yes, of course," said Mrs. Rose. She knew all about worrying, How thought.

"I'm sure Anna's all right," he said awkwardly, stepping back from the doorstep. "I mean—I expect she'll be home soon."

"Yes," said Mrs. Rose. Her fingers fumbled with the handkerchief.

"I'll come tomorrow," How said, "if that's all right."

"It will be very nice," she said. "Thank you."

He walked down the path and, as he turned to latch

the gate, she was still standing on the step, watching him.

How knew he would be lucky to get back before dark. The sky was still luminous above the trees but, from inside a house, it would already seem more like night than day. Auntie Kath was going to be cross.

He ran back along the path the way he had come and glanced automatically toward the old house as he came to the fallen tree. Then he stiffened with shock.

A light gleamed across the garden in the gathering darkness, square and distinct. It came, he knew at once, from behind the half-open door in the old house. He scrambled across the fallen tree toward it, his feet slipping on the muddy bark. If Anna was there, he had to see her. He fought down a sense of disappointment in finding that it was, after all, Anna who had set the telltale light in the house.

Or was it? He stopped, crouching on the tree. What if it was Billy Thrower and the gang? Could they have been stupid enough to set up a dangerous light, hoping for some spiteful reason that Anna and her mother would be blamed for it? That was a disappointing idea as well. Billy was rough and reckless, and he had some crazy ideas, but How had never thought he would do anything as serious as this.

Moving cautiously, he crept to the end of the tree trunk and jumped down into the tangled garden, then made his way carefully toward the house.

There was a rush of footsteps behind him. How jumped around to face his attackers, but it was too late. They were on him, and their combined weight sent him crashing to the ground.

"What d'you think you're doing?" Billy Thrower hissed in his ear. "Was it you set that light in there?"

"No," protested How, struggling. " 'Course not. Get off. Don't be so stupid."

"Who did it, then?" whispered Roger. "Come on— you know, don't you? That's why you're here."

"You want your head examined," How muttered furiously. "I saw the light and thought *you* put it there. I was just going to look around the door and find out."

They hauled him to his feet. "We'll *all* look," said Billy. "Come on."

Holding How's arms firmly, they crept toward the illuminated doorway. This was terrible, How thought. If it was Anna, she would think he was in with Billy's gang. For a moment, he had a wild hope that it might not be Anna. Some tramp, perhaps, seeking shelter for the night? Oh, God, he prayed, let it be a tramp.

Outside the door, Billy paused. "Ready?" he breathed to the gang. They nodded silently.

"*Go!*" said Billy.

Dragging How with them, they burst into the lit room. Someone stood with his back to them, silhouetted against the candlelight, looking down at the old brick bread oven where the ram's skull stood. He turned, unhurried. "Oh, hello," he said.

It was Digger Bailey.

"Digger!" How gasped.

"Told you I got a special place," said Digger, smiling. "That's the old head what I gave Anna. Looks right pretty there. I brought some more candles, see?"

How groaned. "Of *course*," he said. And he knew now where he had seen the corroded dagger blade that lay in front of the ram's skull—on the bench in Mr. Bailey's shed. Now, in addition, there were several neatly arranged coins and, in pride of place, the beaded black silk bag.

"Well, if that don't beat all," said Billy.

They let How's arms go and stood looking at each other.

"I'll shut the door," said Roger, "before anyone else sees the light."

He turned toward the door, and, for the second time, How gasped. Anna was standing in the doorway, her face white in the glimmering candlelight. Above the almost invisible black coat, she seemed like a small, disembodied moon. "So it was you," she said. She came into the room and stared around at them all, but her eyes darted away from How as if she did not want to see that he was there. Roger tugged the door shut, rasping across the brick floor on its sagging, rusted hinges.

Digger smiled at Anna in recognition. "Hello," he said. "Look, I got a pretty thing!" And he pointed to the black silk bag.

"Yes," said Anna kindly. Then she turned on Billy Thrower in a blaze of fury. "Fancy bringing poor Digger into it," she said. "I suppose you thought that was clever. You wanted to get someone into trouble, didn't you—either me and my mother or him. Why are you so—so unkind?" And suddenly her face crumpled and she was crying. Angrily, she shouted through her tears, "You're happy now, aren't you?"

"That's not right!" protested Billy, and the other boys shuffled their feet awkwardly.

Digger gazed at Anna. "Don't cry," he entreated. He looked on the verge of tears himself.

How went across to Anna. "It's all right," he said. "It's not the way you think. Honestly."

"And what are *you* doing," she retorted, still crying, "with *them*?"

"We grabbed him outside," Billy told her. "It's not his fault. He just came to see why the light was showing. And that's why we came, too. We wanted to find out what really was going on, so we came up here, just at dusktime." He shrugged and added honestly, "It could have been you and your mum. But it wasn't. It was Digger."

"My special place," said Digger, smiling again as Anna fished for a handkerchief and blew her nose. "My dad got fed up with things in his shed. I'm going to bring them here."

"You see?" Billy said to Anna.

"Yes," said Anna in a small voice. "I got it all wrong." She gave Billy a tremulous smile and added, "I'm glad, really."

Billy grinned and said, "We're glad, too."

"But where did you go?" How asked Anna. In front

of the boys, he could not mention the hayloft, but he said, "I came looking for you, but you weren't there."

"I know," said Anna. "I heard you. And then I saw you from the window. I hid"—and she glanced at the boys—"in the corner."

Under the hay, thought How, and could have kicked himself for not realizing it before. She was in the hayloft all the time, hiding like a mouse. He felt oddly hurt that she should have hidden from him.

"You had somebody with you," said Anna in accusation. "A soldier."

"He was my *father*," said How.

Anna shrugged apologetically and said, "I didn't know."

Billy and the other boys exchanged puzzled glances as Anna stared at How and continued their private conversation. "What about you?" she asked. "Did the angel work for you in London?"

For a moment, How remembered the dreadful moment when he had stood by the ruins of his house and wept. Then he thought of his mother's narrow escape, and of his own lucky journey, and of the plans for the future. He looked at Anna, and nodded gravely. "Oh, yes," he said. "He worked wonderfully."

There was a tremendous amount to tell her—but suddenly Mrs. Rose was in his mind, standing on her step and watching him as he went down the path. "Your mother's ever so worried," he said. "I've just seen her. I went to your house to see if you were back—that's why I happened to come past here."

"You mean she's back?" said Anna excitedly. "They've let her go?"

"She's been home since lunchtime," said Billy. "Couldn't prove nothing. Well, I mean," he added, "we all know that, don't we?"

"I mucked out the pigs this afternoon," said Digger, who had obviously not been listening, and everyone laughed.

With one of her quick darts, Anna was at the door, dragging it open. "See you at school tomorrow," she said to How over her shoulder, and disappeared into the darkness. How ran to stare out after her, but she had gone as silently as an owl flies. A small, white moon hung in the sky. How pushed the door shut again and turned back to the others. They were all looking at him.

"Funny girl," said Billy innocently.

How looked him in the eye. "From now on," he said, "things have got to be different. You've given her a really bad time, and it's got to stop."

"Oh, yes?" said Billy with a half-hearted attempt at bravado. "Who says?"

"I do," said How.

Billy pushed his hands in his pockets and shrugged, and everyone grinned sheepishly. After a pause, Harry Doggett said, "What was all that about London? Is that where you went? There was an awful fuss about you running away."

"Sorry about that," said How casually. "I just popped down to London to see if everyone was all right."

There was a stunned silence, then Eric Figg said, "I ain't never been to London."

"You came on my bike," put in Digger suddenly, with a broad smile, "when I went to football."

"That's right," agreed How. "And then I stowed away in a coal car."

The boys were staring at him in astonishment and, How realized, with a new respect. But he must not appear to be boasting. Nobody liked people who boasted. He shrugged and said, "It's not difficult to go to London. Traveling's quite easy. You just—go. It's not nearly as difficult as swinging on that bar out there." He nodded toward the door that led out to the hall and the stairwell. "I was scared stiff of that," he added. "But you do it all the time."

There was a very long pause. The boys shuffled and grinned at each other, then Billy Thrower took a deep breath and said, "We never done it. You were the first. That's why the bar bent. I don't reckon any of us ever will, either."

How stared at them and felt his knees turn to water at the thought of what he had so unwittingly dared to do. Then he laughed and shook his head, as the boys watched him and grinned. He had been even more lucky than he had thought.

Eric Figg cast a nervous glance at the ivy-covered window and said, "I'd better go home. I'm not supposed to be out after dark."

"Nor me," said How. The angel was on its way to

London now, in his father's pocket, and there was nothing to protect him from Auntie Kath's fury. "My aunt will skin me alive," he added.

"No, she won't," said Billy stoutly. "We'll all come with you and explain. And Digger, too. Come on, Digger."

"Where?" asked Digger, looking alarmed.

How smiled at him reassuringly. "It's all right," he said. "There's a few things to explain, that's all. A bit of business to sort out."

"Oh," said Digger, smiling back. "Good."

They blew the candles out one by one, until they were in darkness, but the house was not frightening. How felt a sudden surge of excitement at the thought that he might one day live here. Perhaps the house already knew it, he thought. They hauled the door open and went out into the jungly garden.

Billy Thrower, at How's side, nudged him and pushed a small, crumpled paper bag into his hand. It felt hard.

"What is it?" asked How, looking down in the faint moonlight.

"Peppermint drops," muttered Billy. "Don't let the others know."

"Thanks!" said How.

Ahead of them, they could just see the dark shapes of the other boys persuading Digger across the fallen tree. Billy paused. "I've still got some of your sweet coupons left," he said. "Do you want to buy them back?"

How thought briefly. "No," he said. "You keep them. Oh, and I owe you a halfpenny." He fished a coin out of his pocket and gave it to Billy. "You can sell me a bar of chocolate sometimes," he added.

"Right," said Billy. "It's a deal."

They shook hands on the bargain, and How offered him the crumpled paper bag. Billy dug in it for a drop and said, "Thanks."

How took one as well, then pushed the bag into his pocket as he set out beside Billy, across the dark garden. The peppermint drop tasted wonderful. And, somehow, he didn't think Auntie Kath would be too cross, after all.